TREVOR WATTS

Roads Less Travelled
Copyright © 2021 by Trevor Watts.

Dedicated to Chris Watts, for her editing skills, commitment and unending tolerance.

Log on to https://www.sci-fi-author.com/
Facebook at Creative Imagination

First Printing: 2021
Brinsley Publishing Services

BPS

ISBN: 9798705317370

CONTENTS |

CONTENTS II

GET'EM ALL, DAD.

'Omigod, the traffic! Nightmare time. This is ridiculous. It's been hours.' I'm going frantic trying to get there.

'Get a move on,' I bellow out to the assles in front. 'Ten times the traffic and problems, today of all days. It's never been this bad along here before.'

A sea of vehicles in every direction. All squeezing and jostling to get ahead of everyone else.

'Calm down, Jeff. Keep your cool.'

'It's alright for you to stay cool. *You're* not doing the driving. The day's been awful enough without all this to finish it off. They're all imbeciles. Look at *him*, trying to cut in from the side road. He can wait for a proper gap like everybody else. And *that* dickhead's going to let that van in. *Idiot,'* I yelled out the window.

'Do it, Dad! Get'em all!' I got super-supportive kids in the back. They understand these things.

'Jeff, you'll have an apoplexy, relax a—'

'How can I—? *Go for it...!* That's it – stop him. Don't let that one in...' I'm muttering to myself and ranting out the window at the other traffic.

And Rowena's beside me non-sympathising with my plight in this heart-attack-inducing chaos. 'Gently, dear, we'll get there.' She's no help at all.

'We don't want to be stuck behind that soddin' minibus...'

'Get him, Dad!' At least the kids were rooted in on my side – no traitors in the back. 'Get'em all.'

'Oh my God, no wonder it's so slow today – one lane's coned off. What the hell for? Nobody working, of course.'

1

'Typical, innit, Dad?'

'Stone the crows, they're all coming round the mini-island. They've cut through the pub yard and trying to force back in. That's it – block the buggers off – they gain twenty car lengths doing that.'

'Not on my dad, you don't!' Katie's leaning out the window in full support, too. 'You're not pushing in front of us.'

'Come on, come on, get a move on. How long does it take, you lard-brained toad? We've been bloody hours stuck on this road.'

'Jeff! You nearly—'

'He'll live.'

'Get this next one as well, Dad.'

'Mind him, Dad. He's trying to chop in.'

'Not this close, he isn't.'

'Talk about a white-knuckle ride, Jeff. It's been—'

'Thank God for that… Us next.'

Great… Ease forward at last…

Handbrake on. Head out the window.

An over-bright face at the end of all that torment. Have they no sense of the suffering we've been through to get here? Grinning like a moron, eyebrows raised in query.

'Get'em all, Dad,' I heat from behind me.

I took a deep breath and let it all out:

'Two Canadian stacks.

And three Big Macks.

All with fries.

And seven cokes, the giant size.

A Double Quarter Pounder with extra mayo and melted cheese.

And bacon rolls – the special offer's for packs of threes?

Plus salad for three,

2

And a sharebox filled with cheese and chicken chunks for me.
Five ice cream cones with chocolate flakes, and a salted caramel McFlurry.
And, pleeease – make it *fast* food – we're in a hurry.'

ISOBEL IS WAITING...

Carrie and I had come visiting from England, mostly for an extended holiday in Oz. 'But we'll time it to help with your cross-country move,' we told daughter Isobel.

'I'm not sure if she looked pleased or tolerant,' Carrie said, breaking the Zoom connection.

The way we organised it was for Isobel and I to engage in an easy three-day drive from Izzy's old place to her new home, and new job in New South Wales. 'Big promotion, Dad.'

'You deserve it, lass. Higher than I ever made. Better money, too.' Good girl, my Isobel. The boss, eh?

'It's a fortnight since I finished my post in Perth. I feel like a lady in waiting – as it were. I'll be glad to get started at the new one.'

'Not much more waiting, Izzy. A week Monday, is it? We'll make the most of the time.'

She and I were going to drive cross-country, and open her new house, get it aired, and the furniture arranged how she wanted. Utilities switched on and everything. 'That'll take a couple of days, then Carrie and the toddlers can take the flight to join us. You and I will have spruced the place up, so this'll be our time together, Izzy.'

I'd been looking forward to it; my first opportunity to actually be with her in the two years since she'd moved out here. Especially with her new job coming up – so much to talk about.

To be dead honest, it was great. After an initial hour or two or distant awkwardness, stilted silences, she mentioned some time in the distant past when I'd picked her up, and it had banged her head on an overhead beam and made her nose bleed. She was laughing about it and asking if it had really happened, 'Or is it my imagination?'

'Oh, it's true. I did. You'd let go of your Goose Fair balloon and were crying. I lifted you so you could see it blowing away as long as possible. You got over the balloon pretty quickly after that.'

We were laughing about it for miles and got onto a host of other incidents and half-memories, until the sign across the highway said, "Road closed – Bush Fires – Police".

So we u-turned with the few other vehicles on the road, and called in the police station a mile back. They eventually came to the security window after we'd rung the bell three times. The smartly-uniformed girl sipped her tea. 'No, we have no information on the closures, or where the bush fires are spreading… The troopers are all out. You'll just have to keep an eye out for them.'

'You've been helpfulness personified,' Izzy congratulated her, oozing the sweetest of sarcastic smiles.

The troopers were all out, sure enough. Across the road, at Benny's Café. Six police cars were lined up outside – Ford Falcons and two Toyotas, including a Hilux with a cage trailer. Two two-dozen uniforms occupied all the outside tables of the breakfast and coffee bar.

'Having a well-earned rest, mate…'

'Just coming on duty, mate. Need a caffeine kick-start.'

'I'm not open to the public yet. Be with you in ten…'

'No idea which roads are open, Bluey. There's smoke everywhere. Just drive along'em and see, eh?' Waving us away, enjoying the coffee, the sun, the power over the travelling public.

6

'Pom, are you? The fire lot'll turn you round if you get too far the wrong way... if you're lucky.'

That was a cause for some amusement; 'You're a pack of Pommie-baiters, hmm?'

'Try the mountain road,' one suggested, pointing towards the distant smoke over the far hills.

'Yeah, thanks, we just got turned back from there.'

'You know more than us,' they were laughing and turning away, glancing to see who else was in my car, muttering and commenting.

Sighing, we bought a coffee to go, and decided on the road towards the Ocean Views Highway. The coast road would add a couple of hours on, but it didn't matter. One the officers was on the phone as we drove off; he seemed to be looking at my reg plate, perhaps checking that I hadn't stolen it. Obviously a rental... tourist. Target for fun.

Twenty minutes later, a police car hurtled past us on the way down a long drag. Sure enough, he was round a bend a mile further on, standing in the middle of the road with a speed gun out, waving us down.

Sarcastic, gloating little creature. Swaggering round, all five foot six of him in his blue and sand-coloured uniform with badges scattered round it. 'Yeah, we get loads of you Poms along here. The way we keep changing the limits – every week, every bend, it gets dozens of you.' He was grinning broadly, 'Yeah, dozens.

'Now get the back open.'

'They're just suitcases.'

'Open 'em up.' He scowled. Not the sunny type. The wart on his nose probably didn't help his disposition.

'Come on, we're just—'

'Are you resisting? I ordered you to open them for inspection.' He had his back up now, overtly aggressive.

7

'Where you heading? Where are you staying tonight? When ya flying home?

'Right,' parading round the car twice… and he stood there, middle of the road, writing out a ticket, ringing it in, then turning away, ringing someone else. 'Yeah, these two trappy Poms, I got'em.' A snigger, 'Yeah, some slag sheila with him.'

'Two hundred and sixty dollars!' I couldn't believe the ticket he handed me.

'Oh, yeah, we really sting you over here, Pom. Y' lucky I don't take you down the station and put y' through it. Do all the checks and everything, eh? You'd be there a coupla days. Enjoy that, eh? Miss y' flight then, eh?'

'Come on, what was I doing? It was 45 round the headland; then we were on the straight…'

'Yeah, and the limit drops to 30 on the straight. You were exceeding that.' Ugly smirk, he had. 'We get dozens of you with that.'

'I never even saw another sign. All the other straights have been 55. If there was a sign, there's not enough time to see it and slow down. Seems like the speed limit changes every two hundred yards.'

'Yeah. Like I said, that's the way we get you. We got seventeen speed changes from the river to here. We like to ring in with a few changes every month or so, *Pom*.' That smirk again. 'Two hundred-sixty dollars. Or I can escort you down the station and you pay double there.'

I contented myself by thinking I was on holiday, had had a pretty good time, and would be back in England in a few days, free of this obnoxious little turd. So I smiled and paid in cash.

Back in the car, Izzy congratulated me, 'You're so calm and pleasant; you're taking it so well, dad.'

8

Part of the calming process was to get off the road and have a bite to eat, sit in the sun.

'Ahh. Hello. You're the Pair o' Poms.'

We looked up. Two more police officers, pointing to some graffiti and damage to the little tiles on a mosaic wall next to where we sat. 'You damaged that.' Not a question; it was an accusation.

Of course we denied it. I did anyway. But they were just being awkward, harassing the Pommy tourists for entertainment. 'It shouldn't be there in the first place,' I ventured. 'It's crap workmanship; and there's no way a fish shaped like that ever existed, even in Australia.' That, naturally, didn't go down well and we were advised to move along before we got ourselves into real bother. Pity; it had been very pleasant there in the sun, with the best fish and chips I'd had since leaving England. 'Hi ho, off we go.'

Another ten minutes and we stopped at the Cathedral Cliffs; towering great white walls with enormous caves, huge ocean rollers coming in, and a million gannets wheeling round.

Back at the car, two more of them were waiting for us. They'd had a call come through; our two-sixty dollars had been checked, and some notes were suspected of being from a laundered deal they'd been attempting to trace for some time.

'You're not very good at tracing, then,' I mentioned, showing them the receipt from Currency Exchange International. They studied it, rang through to somewhere, ummed and woofed, and sent us on our way. Pity, we'd fancied an ice cream from the van in the car park.

'I guess they didn't like us asking about the diversion, back at Benny's Café.'

'I think we're the amusement for today. I'll drive for a time, Dad, while you calm down and watch the scenery, take a pic or two.'

Isobel's a good driver; very competent and confident; cruising round a long bend, keeping strictly to the limit, 35... 50... 30... 45... changes every few hundred yards. A huge truck was coming up behind us, flashing. Izzy slowed down and eased over to let him past.

'Silly sod, it's a long bend.' So he was swerving out and tucking back in for a mile or so as the road wound snakelike. Sure, we could have gone faster, but the speed limit was different on every corner and straight. Even a slight uphill had a change of limit half-way up.

The truck was intent on ignoring the limit and the double centre-lines as we attained the top of the rise and started the long easy downhill, swinging out yet again. 'He's determined this time...'

So Izzy took her foot off again to let him do it quickly, 'I'll be glad to be rid of him, Dad. We can call for coffee and a pie at the next place, and let him get well ahead. We'll find a nice picnic spot along the cliffs.'

So this truck with a massive trailer on the back came past us as the road straightened out, and we were doing about twenty by then to let him do it.

Ahh... There was this uniform standing in the middle of the road. The truck had just missed him, but he was still standing there, speed gun aimed at us, swaying a bit from the truck's draught. 'He's focussed on us, alright.' Izzy sighed and pulled up where he was waving us to stop.

He was the same officer as the first pull-up. Grinning little Warty-nose, coming round the driver's side, 'Ah,

10

you again. The little lady driving this time eh? Travelling at an unduly slow and unsafe speed. You really do go for variety, you two, eh? Right. ID, then get out the car, Miss.

A pickup came past, hooting hotly. 'You really should be careful, Officer, he didn't miss you by much.'

'And you, Lady…' He was up in arms now, high dudgeon indeed. 'You don't go telling officers of the law what they should and shouldn't do, Right? You got that? Now do like I said, Get out the car.' He bent down to look inside, and curled a lip at me. 'You too,'

So I climbed out, resigned to it. Warty stood back as Izzy slid sideways and out, leering at her legs as he reached for his cell phone again. 'Stand on the roadside, Miss. I need to ring through and check your ID.' Huge smirk as he had obviously decided that there would be something very wrong with our ID. 'This might take some time.'

Izzy came and joined me on the verge among the busy lizzies and sowthistles. We could hardly see the officer over the top of the car, but he was still strutting round in the middle of the road. I glimpsed the phone at his ear once when he spun round, full of his own importance, and I happened to meet his eyes as he looked in our direction just as something he heard on the phone made him mouth "What?"

Wham!!!

He'd gone.

A blur of truckside. A whoosh of air… long blast of a receding horn. Warty-nose wasn't there any longer.

A 38-tonner semi was pulling up a hundred yards or more down the road, hazard flashers coming on. An awful lot of blood and mashed, rolled-about, flesh and uniform remains were spread along the carriageway…

'What th…'

'Oh shit…'

'Oh God…'

'Yeuk…'

We walked along the road towards the stationary truck. 'He must have got caught in the wheels…'

'...or one of the axles.'

'Lord, the stench of blood.'

'There's not much of him still together…'

Unsteadily, the truck driver was coming towards us, skirting round the scattered splashes and fragments. We met up at the main splurt of gore and shredded clothing.

'Don't worry, driver, we witnessed it, didn't we, Izzy?' She was in shock, staring all along the trail of ex-police officer, her ID lying there in all the blood.

'Yes,' I carried on, 'the officer stepped back, right in front of you. We'll swear to that.'

'Hellfire – so much blood…' The driver was awestricken at the long dark trail that stretched between our vehicles.

I bent to retrieve the blood-dripping ID; offered to her. She shook her head, 'Dad? How am going to face the officers who investigate this mess? and when I turn up at my new job with *that* as my ID?'

I opened it up, 'It's barely readable through all the blood, but don't worry about it. Your street cred will go through the roof if they think this is your idea of discipline before you've even started the job, "Isobel Denver,"' I quoted, '"Senior Commissioner of Police. NSW".'

LAST MINUTE LIZZIE

It's as if I'm always reluctant to part with anything, including myself. I always leave it to the last moment to do anything, especially giving something up. It's a compulsion with me, I suppose.

'It's mine,' I said when the teachers insisted I give my homework in. 'It's not ready for your eyes... just a few more points I thought of—' before they usually snatched it off me, or put me in detention for it being late.

Same with my 6th form essay competition entry. It was the close of school on the last possible day and I caught Mr Jeeves on his way to his car, 'There were a couple more paras to polish,' I said.

My application for the job at MyMag was so very nearly late arriving. I hand-delivered it, all the way down to Nottingham. It was too brilliantly phrased to trust it to the Post Office. It said such lovely things about me. 'Simply needed a few extras adding,' I told the man on the front desk as he was attempting to close everything down.

Then when I had Jenny, I went full term, and past it... a couple of weeks and I lied about the due date, but Hubby knew and wasn't going to let me get away with it, so he phoned and got me in and induced. 'I only wanted another day or two,' I wailed. Then when I was in, it took thirteen hours in labour, three doses of oxytocin, sticking something up me to break my waters, and a few more pushes.

'Looks like Moses has been here,' Hubby said, 'I'm practically paddling.'

My first book was pretty much the same. I was never quite, fully, completely, absolutely happy with it. There was always a para to change, a different twist, alter someone's name... and the title never seemed quite right.

'I sent it off this morning,' Hubby said. 'While you were at work. I simply pressed the "Publish" button on KDP. It's been waiting for three weeks.'

I cried to lose it, 'I had a super new inspiration for page 99,' I told him, really a bit cross.

He was another one: when he proposed. It was in that fabulous Mexican diner in Mansfield – Chiquito's, and he was on the floor on his knees. The waitress kept offering to pick something up if he'd dropped a nachos or a quesadilla or something, 'Just leave it, and I'll bring you another.'

They're awfully helpful in there. But it was so hard to decide, and it took me all evening and I said, 'You'd better sit back up and finish your tortillas before your chimichangas go off.'

I knew I'd say, "Yes" but it was just finding the right tone of voice and expression, as well as actually summoning up the courage to say it. So he sat up and I said, 'I'll text you before the meal's over.'

'Well, I meant before we'd finished the pina coladas,' I told him. 'Or before we went to bed.'

But he said, 'I'll take it as a "yes",' and we went to bed anyway.

And I said, 'Alright then,' when he laid his hands on me.

And now this has to happen...

They keep wanting me to go for psychiatric therapy to combat procrastination – although I haven't made up mind about what they mean exactly, and whether or not I ought to go. I said, 'I'll think about it while we're on holiday.'

It wasn't me who booked Tenerife; it was Hubby. But I couldn't choose, and it was getting near the time he'd booked time off, so he said, 'Executive decision.' And tossed a coin. 'It's Tenerife,' he said, and was on the phone straight away. Pre-empting my objections.

'There's something about Tenerife I don't like,' I told the girls. 'I can't remember what.'

'You'll think of something, mum,' Lily, Lexi and Lucy assured me.

'I prefer Lanzarote because there's a super beach and fun park that we loved last time, didn't we?' I sort of got it on me and didn't know if I really wanted to go at all because me and Lily looked like we had a bad cold coming on. I was packing and unpacking and I was being slow about deciding what to take and hoping maybe it would be too late and we'd miss the plane or something.

'Well, there's something about it I'm not fond of,' I told Hubby for the umpteen trillionth time, when he threw my suitcase in the car boot and started the engine up.

But he had to turn it off again while I searched for the passports. And I just got in the car when I remembered the money and just couldn't find it anywhere. It was in my handbag when he looked again.

'If we miss that blasted plane—' he said. Very ominously.

We did. I felt really awful about it and the kids were blaming me, too. I felt so guilty – I was guilty. And I felt it. "Stupid co… moo,' he called me. Right there in the airport. 'It's every chuffing time,' really emphasising every word so everybody could tell he was cross with me. 'Knew you'd push it too far one day.'

Course, I was everso sorry and saying, 'I don't know what came over me, pushing it so close. Sorry... sorreee...'

'Too effing close. Effing ell.' He went stalking off with the kids to the desk to see if there was another flight in that direction today... or somewhere else warm and nice, "With single beds," he specified, and stared at me very hard when I caught them up with all the baggage on our trolley and a nice man who came to help me when he saw me trying to decide whether to cry or get mad.

Yes, they did have another flight going out today, with room on for all of us. I was almost sorry about that, but thought it was probably best not to say anything because I wanted to stay married after all that bother at the altar those times before.

'It's to somewhere just as wonderful and warm and fun-for-children,' the very smartly-uniformed lady very reassuringly said, and gave Li, Le and Lu a lollipop each. He treated me to a look like a macaroni mackerel. 'This alternative place is not four-star, but it has a very individual rating, and its own little beach. It works out less expensive, because it's filling the flight, and some stand-by people had your seats and room in Playa de las Américas. So,' she summed up, 'I can put you on this one to Marbella with no extra charge, yes?'

'Yes.'

'Yes.'

'Yes.'

'Yes.' They said in age order.

'Er,' I said, and felt the icy blast from them all. 'Er, I mean, er... what time does it take off?'

'Midnight, arriving 3.30. Two-hour transfer time.'

'Midnight? That's... It's... er... six o'clock now... Er... six hours waiting here.' Lucy wasn't too quick with numbers.

So we settled in the lounge. Or unsettled in it: I was fretting, naturally, about whether to go to the toilet or the book shop, and if I delayed it too long, which would I regret the most?

They were all complaining aloud or under their breaths. My own kids! So snidey. Even they were calling me names. Hubby had a drink... and another. I didn't dare count or say anything, but it was five. He wasn't saying anything at all, but he was muttering a lot. And mumbling. A fair bit of twitching and pacing, too. Plus the glaring looks.

'Well, I don't know,' I said. 'I didn't really fancy Tenerife, anyway. I bet Ma Bella's just as good, if not better, wherever it is. There was just something about Tener— Oh. What's going on down there? See? Something's come up on the screens. All the people pointing?'

We looked, but couldn't see that far away. Definitely something on the screens... and someone coming out to talk to people down there.

'I'll go see,' Hubby soured at me. 'Get another drink while I'm up.'

'Are you sure? It's nearly time to be going to the gate and—' But he'd gone.

He took his time, and the girls were quiet with me. All blame and lollipops. There were people near us who were going to see as well.

We'd finished our lollipops by the time he came back. I was going to say had he changed his mind about a drink, or the flight.

He was all shaking and just stood there. His mouth was working. He was crying.

'Daddy...?'

'Our plane... to Tenerife. It crashed. Landing at Reina Sofía airport. It's in flames. Blew up. Exploded on the runway. There's a vid of it... They don't think there's any chance of survivors.'

I was frozen up, just listening, and looking up at him, standing there shaking and tears pouring. I stood up and wanted him to sit down with me, 'Come on, Love,' I'm telling him, 'Sit yourself down... come on. I'll get that drink.'

He wouldn't. He just put his arms round me, and hugged and hugged and hugged me, and I was getting all wet and soggy. 'I promise... I'll never call you again. No more Last-Minute Lizzie.'

THE A42

'For the love of Mike, get off my tail.'

I'm driving my Toyota HiAce van, practically nothing in the back, so it's not like I'm weighed-down and holding anything up.

'I'm looking in the mirror more than I'm seeing what's ahead,' I'm chuntering away at him. 'This's the A42, not Brand's Hatch.' Yet another quick glance at the moron right behind me. A Volkswagen T-Roc by the look of it. 'And it's not the Nürburgring, either.' I mean, if you're going to get a German car, at least make it a decent one – like a Merc SLK.

Coming up so close behind me, I can't even see him out the back windows. Then he's dropping back and charging close again. Sheer intimidation tactics. Lights flashing. 'Ha! Trying to bully Big White Van Man? You've got no chance, mate. I see a thousand like you every day. There's nowhere I can go,' I'm mumbling to myself, getting more irate with him that I usually do with prats. 'We're in the outside lane, of two.'

I've been overtaking a stream of lorries, artics and builders' open-backs, for miles. And, of course, they're doing fifty-five – sixty, same as always along here. You get one lorry pull out, doing one mph faster than the nerk in front, and it holds up the outside lane for ten minutes.

'For chuff's sake, stay back. We're in a queue. You *can't* get past. There's nowhere to go, you berk.'

If I could have let the idiot past, I would have done, but there were two dozen cars and vans in front of me; and the same on my left. Solid traffic; all doing the same speed. Plus a couple of HGVs that had taken their chance to force their way out.

'Okay,' I'm thinking, 'maybe you're too stupid to look past me and see it's the same in front. Still, soon as I can, I'll let you past. I'd rather have you in front of me than up my backside flashing like a raincoat on Hampstead Heath. You never know,' I'm muttering, 'I suppose you might be the fuzz, desperate to get to your tea break.'

Yeah, some dick in front of me was suddenly pulling out. Big lorry. You leave enough safety room in front and somebody'll fill the gap. That left a space next to me. 'Here you go, Racer Boy,' I said to myself, and I dabbed the signal and swung over, into the "slow" lane. 'Come on past, you impatient turd. You'll get all of thirty yards ahead.'

Except, the dick-of-a-lorry who'd pulled out slammed his brakes on, great strip of lights down each side of the back unit. Whole line of red tail lights ahead of him.

So VW's showing his acceleration off, and he comes hurtling past me. For all of a van's length. Straight into to the back of this stationery lorry.

**

'No, Officer, it hadn't actually stopped, it wasn't *stationary*. It was a *stationery* lorry – WH Smith. Yes, after that, it was stationary too – it had a VW stuck pretty solidly up its backend.'

PASS ME BY

'Oh, great, the chuffing thing.' Totally at a loss for what might be wrong with the half-acre of electronics, I dropped the bonnet back in place, and tried the ignition once more. The dashboard lit up, all the dials and readouts in red for a moment, then switched itself off. 'Dead.' And the phone might as well be – no reception at all.

I climbed out, sagged against the car. 'The amount I paid to rent this heap for a month. I've been done.' Quick look round the car park – more of a view-point pull-in at the top of a mountain pass, almost deserted now.

Towards evening, a couple of dozen people watching the sunset; all leaving now. There was only one other vehicle left, a tourist coach. I went to see if they'd give me a lift down to the nearest garage or town.

'Nu. La dracu. Străin.' I know dracu is obscene; the rest, I could guess. The driver wrinkled his nose, curled his lips, and started up with a turn of the key. A casual two-fingered gesture, and the coach edged forward. Other passengers stared silently. One smiled and waved. Kids with tongues stuck out.

'Shugger.' More than a mite chalked off, but not too much – you always survive, don't you? Something to tell'em when you get back. Except... not a lot to bother getting back to this time.

'Wind's picking up. Temperature's dropping. It's too exposed up here, even in the car.' It was getting dark, but there was moonlight, so I decided to walk down. 'Might be a shelter, or car passing. Or roadside house, café. Farm barn... Anything out the cold and wind, really. So, big

21

coat on, couple of bars of chocolate in the pockets, gloves… keys… bobble-hat. And I started down the hill.

Hill? 2323 metres, the sign at the pull-in said. 'That's seven thousand feet – twice the height of anything in England.'

Within ten minutes, the road surface was turning slippy, icy. Gleaming in the moonlight. Snow settling in – wind stronger. 'I'm not wrapped too well here,' I realised, but it was too late to head back to the car. The moon vanished as a black snowstorm took over. Almost totally dark, it wasn't safe to walk. The snow was deepening so fast. Using the phone light occasionally – still no reception – I tried to follow the road, mostly looking for the least sign of a shelter, rock, heap of hay, anything I could crawl under. And I was getting real feelings of *I shouldn't have done this… This is serious…*

'Ahh. There!' A light, perhaps a few hundred yards away from the road. Hard to tell the distance in the darkness and blizzarding snow. 'Have to try to get over the fields to it. Be alright.'

Over a stone wall. Dropped. Further than I'd imagined. Big fall into a snowdrift… struggling out of it onto frozen grass and mud, rocks. 'Shuggs – I'm really stuck.' Another quick flash of the cell-phone. Could be a steep downhill over moorland. I went… stumbling, freezing, kinda scared. Not desperate about it. Another stone wall. I'm frozen stiff by then.

Scramble over the wall. 'The light's gone. Shuggit! So now you're totally lost and frozen.' There was something there. Something alive. Goats? Not cattle – not big enough. Sheep? Probably – thick and woolly. My fingers were too far gone to do anything, so I forced in among them, and curled up, forcing my hands up inside my coat,

22

and waited. And froze. *Shuggs... this is how bodies get found weeks later, in spring.*

Shuddering all night in the shelter of the wall. 'It's alright for you sheep – they got thicker coats that me.' Perished through. No feeling other than dull pain in my feet, I woke up completely buried in drifted snow. Forcing to my feet, head poking out, I was in a stone-walled sheep fold, shaped like a swastika to give some shelter whatever the wind direction. Yep – a dozen or so snowy mounds surrounded me – sheep.

A croft was there, tiny, boarded roof-planks sticking out from beneath three feet of snow... and overhanging drifts of the same depth. Perhaps two hundred yards away. I fell, staggered towards it... Got stopped by a ravine with rocky, half-frozen stream. 'Ahh, lucky. A two-plank bridge, all iced and treacherous and heaped with a foot of snow. Frozen and shuddering up the steep bank the other side, the snow had drifted deeper. *There's no help out here... I'm not going to survive, my toes are solid, must be dead and white.*

A face at a tiny, almost iced-over window, peeking between the drifted snow and the down-hanging snow from the roof. The mouth moved. It vanished. Some scuttering at a deep-recessed door further along. I clawed and staggered sideways. Into a partial porch. The door struggled open. Bony hands reaching at me. 'Thank God.' I was falling inward, being heaved and dragged. The door forcing to. People pulling at me; moving the in-fallen snow away. A fire. So dim. So warm. A ring of pale faces.

Pulling at my frozen clothes... shoes... more muttering than talking. Not English. Prematurely aged, weather-beaten couple with silent staring kids... Lying near-naked by the fire, fresh-warmed rough blankets laid over me

23

from time to time. Feet held, wrapped, massaged. The children did that in turn – their job for the day, evening, however long it took for the frozen blocks to turn to agonising screaming feet and writhing rest of me. Shuggerty! It hurt so much.

They peered and felt and poked, and mumbled at me, my toes were all still there. Still whitish, no blackness of frostbite. I spluttered at some awful, so-welcome brew of grease and fat, so scalding hot. Maybe lamb with offal... called Drob, I think. Loaded with spices – basil and allspice, I thought, and didn't care.

I was moved away from the fire, re-covered in blankets stuffed with hay, and supplied with endless jugs of the Drob – definitely offal – liver was the most obvious-tasting ingredient, but there was chopped intestine and heart – *atrial valve there,* I recognised. *Tastes okay.*

Warm, peat fire, no English. Laugh at the idea of a phone, or reception. I showed mine. They turned it over a few times, shrugged and handed me a pot of warm water and a thunk of black pikelet bread. A strip of smoked meat to chew on. Can't stop shaking. More gruel – they seemed to regard me as the idiot child who didn't know any better than to be caught outside in a blizzard. But were tolerant.

Two days? Three? All together in the room, plus a litter of piglets that strayed in from a back room. And some goats. And chickens that roosted in the rafters. No wonder it was warm. Fuggy and richly smelling. Five children I guessed, but they didn't hold still, and looked similar, just different sizes, and presumably ages. Plus two baby-toddler-size beings.

They brought the sheep into a covered shed lean-to out the back. It took all day. Wouldn't let me help – dismissed the idea with a wave and a laugh.

Petru disappeared for a day. Returning before dark, he and Maria conveyed that the pass was closed – hard ice and deep drifting snow. So I'm stuck there, still shuddering with cold deep inside, even after how many days? Not so bad, I thought. *Not so bad??!!* It's effing wonderful! I'm alive. Warming up. No worries to speak of. Five kids who are fantastic little humourists – they think I'm funny, anyway. We pull faces, sing songs, play jokes on each other, mess up the mat-weaving and hook-rug-making. Actually, I was okay at the rug-making. They just weren't keen on my idea of patterns. And I could pluck some peculiar guitar called, I think, a cobza. Battered and not my idea of being in tune, but what the eff? They made sounds to some folksy Spinners and Seekers ones I know, and I entertained them with my joining-in with theirs.

The oldest one was a girl with a sad-smiley face. Or serious-smiley, more like. Mihaela. I especially warmed to her.

Some veg to chew, cold salted bacon, and liquor from a chipped enamel pail kept the evenings going. Chocolate! I remembered. Two blocks to break up and share out over four evenings. Faces of delight, me included.

I was promoted to a bed – sort of. A thick heap of stuffed mattresses. It was shared. With lice, rats and something wormy. But you pick them off in the morning and get dressed. Also shared with two of the children. You have to pick them off, as well. Lack of space and the need to share warmth was the reason there. They didn't say anything about cutting bits off me if I touched the kids, and it wasn't even implicit: it hadn't occurred to

25

them. It did to me, in a fearful negative way – suppose they thought I did? Suppose I had an accidental touch? Or brush? I slept in dread of some misconstruing and kept very still all night, hugging my hands close to me.

The children weren't bothered: I think they dossed down wherever the fancy took them, in different combinations. They'd snuggle close for warmth, or just foreign-ness. And I'd wake up, almost terrified at the feel of an arm across me, or a small bare backside pressed against me. Or in utter fear that I'd wake up with an erection – I would die. God! If Mihaela saw. But it was warm, and it helped to keep the clothing vermin-free, hanging in front of the fire.

Excitement. A helicopter came hovering above the croft. Petru and Maria waved and brought me out for them to see, but I doubt anyone understood anything. I wasn't totally entranced at the idea of so-called rescue.

Later, another, larger one, came lower, swooping and exploring the slopes. Petru, heavily-clad, went out. He returned after a couple of hours. A neighbour had heard on a radio that a tourist coach was missing. The kids drew pictures to show me. Maybe the same coach I saw on top of the pass?

The blizzard returned, blustering, with deeper drifting. No more helicopters for four days – must be grounded in the renewed blizzard. I imagined search parties struggling in the snow, then looked out the window again, and decided that wasn't happening. Completely snowed in – ten-foot drifts in the valley bottoms and edges of roads, in the lee where the wind dropped and so did the snow.

They opened the road after three weeks – the snow had been *deep*, for mile after mile up the road, and they extracted me after four weeks, amazed to find me alive. All a rush and whirling blades and no real goodbyes and I was gone – such a rush they were in.

Someone had taken my car down when the pass was clear, and it had been reclaimed by the rental agency. They fixed the problem – engine management chip failed. I was presumed lost and dead, but I've had a check-up – no long-term debility, so I'm free to go and collect my baggage out the car, and do whatever; continue my vacation, or try to get on a flight home.

Home. Huh.

The coach was found a couple of days later – upside down in a ravine, rolled several times and completely crushed and smashed up. There was a lot about it on the television and the local newspaper. It looks like an iced bend, like every other, and the coach simply didn't make it – rushing to get down to the hotel for the check-in and evening meal. Skidded sideways, and the wheels hit the low stone barrier wall side-on, and slammed sideways over the wall, and rolled down a steep rocky slope, demolishing a dozen pine trees, and landing upside-down in a ravine. All were dead by then, probably, but the coach half-blocked the ravine, and the freezing water ponded back, overflowed, and poured through the remains of the coach. There wasn't much sight of it under the heavy snow shroud, even where the trees had gone – it was deep, deep white everywhere. The ravine was thirty or forty feet deep and the snow had filled it.

Staying in Necu for a time – "resting" officially. More like "no idea what to do or where to go-ing". I keep thinking about it all.

What I keep thinking… that driver who V-signed me on his way out the car park at the top – he's dead now, but I still keep seeing his sneer. I don't mind he did that. I didn't then – I remember shrugging and thinking it was my own fault – or at least, it was on me, not him. So what did he get punished for? Same with the pair of revolting kids sticking their tongues out. They didn't deserve that; they must have screamed and screamed until they were smashed up, or drowned trapped in their holiday coach. I keep imagining the awful scene there must have been inside the coach that the recovery people had to work through. *I'm* having nightmares – the recovery team must be on their mental knees. I could really weep for them.

I'm thinking, the best I've felt lately was in that tiny stone croft with Petru and Maria and the family and their livestock. Not from the relief I felt, thinking I was likely going to survive – by then I hadn't felt too bothered that my time had come. But I'd just loved every minute in there, even the agony of defrosting on warm gruel and a peat fire; lying with goats and sheep; and warming myself on five kids' smiles and laughs and songs and teasing me. I didn't have anything to worry and complicate my mind about. It seemed so simple then; and bereft of pain. Lacking hassle.

So I'm planning on going back up there to see if they'll let me help around for a time, maybe I can help fix the boarding on the roof – some roofing felt, perhaps; and get the back door fitting right again. Maybe rebuild the sheepfold with some fresh-bought timber. Ask if they want any different food stocks or clothes. Possibly help with getting some tools, medications for livestock… whatever. If they'll let me.

I can't leave this region yet, this country, these people. I've been through too much here to simply clear off. I'd be leaving something of myself here. I need to get it settled within myself. Bit of peace inside. I'm thinking I'll stay as long as I need to, if they'll allow me in. Perhaps long enough to learn sufficient of their dialect to actually speak with Mihaela.

After all, I got nothing to go back to now, since Vanessa… The rest of the world can pass me by, too.

To seal it, I just managed to get hold of eight bars of Cadbury's Dairy Milk. Mihaela really loved that.

MY THERAPIST SAYS

It's seven miles – twenty-five minutes – to work in the car every day. My therapist says I should always leave early, and have plenty of time. 'Take it easy; no rush.' She's very reassuring.

Check my hair a few times... nails... a few lip-glossy pouts and purses into the mirror. *'Bellissima,'* I congratulated myself. My therapist says I should always be confident in my appearance. So I have to check frequently – every half-mile.

'Merda!' A car. Huge midnight blue thing hurtled in front of me from the outside lane at forty-five degrees. Smashing into the back of the rather nice silver-bronze estate car I was behind. Lord, my heart was fluttering and thumping like a dozen butterfly elephants. I sagged down. *'Dio!'* Thank God – it missed my front wing by inches. Oh, thank God again.

A bit wobbly, I got out and waved the following cars into the outside lane to come past us. I thought I'd better wait there and see if anyone was hurt... or needed an ambulance to be called... be a witness, and all that sort of thing. I've seen it on the telly, so I know what I ought to do.

They seemed to be uninjured, if really mad with each other. The driver of the estate car at the front came to me, all bothered and angry. He wanted to know if I saw it... my name... going where?

Then the other one came, from the dark blue car. He was bigger and even angrier. And louder, 'You, you little cow. What you stopped for? Nothing to do with you, is it? Go on, bugger off. Mind your own business.' I mean, I

31

felt really threatened as he came leaning over me, 'You didn't see anything, did you? And who are you? Address?'

My therapist says I should always remain calm. 'Count to ten... or a hundred if the occasion warrants it,' she said. I got to fifty-five before I said, 'My name is MiaLuce Tesore. Here's my card. Yes, I did see what happened.' I stood at my full five-foot-three, 'and I'm prepared to swear to it in court.'

'MiaLuce what? Foreign, are you? Wet your drawers, have you?'

'You horrible man,' I told him. 'And no – I haven't. Thank you for enquiring.'

I was very glad when he backed up and drove off, waving and cursing at everyone. He swore at me quite a lot before he left. So I finished my vanilla coffee and took my Valium and calmed down in ten minutes with the breathing control routine my therapist taught me.

The driver from the first car was nice to me, although he was very angry, until I pointed to my windscreen and the dash cam mounted on it. 'It's working, and it's switched on,' I told him. 'And he definitely ran into you.'

He was Mr Morton, and he worked in an office in town. I thought he was going to kiss me. I don't do that on the street, even if I am half Italian, *grazie a Dio*.

I made a few copies for myself at work and posted the original to him. It was easier and quicker to send the whole ninety-minute chip, rather than sort out which bit of which three-minute file the bump was on. It all had the times on, so they'd be able to find it easily enough.

**

He phoned a few weeks later: 'My insurance company appreciates the footage very much, but they're getting nowhere with the other driver or his insurance company.

32

We suspect the driver was drunk, and may have connections with the police, from the way we're being blocked.

'My insurance is pressing for charges of reckless or dangerous driving to be brought against him,' he said, 'but Royal and Domestic are up against a brick wall. The police are being obstructive, refusing to act on anything, claiming the footage can't be verified, not the place or the time or the vehicles or the drivers. They're trying to claim that I stopped dangerously and deliberately reversed into him.'

'*Idioti.*'

**

Then the police arrived in person at my little home. Two of them; a sergeant and a constable. Brusque, they demanded the chip with the original recording on it.

'No. I don't have to give you anything. Go away or I'll call the police.' I stamped my Jimmy Choos, and turned my back on them.

So they threatened to charge me with obstructing a police investigation... defraud of an insurance company... perverting the course of justice – tampering with evidence. They were throwing accusations at me like concrete confetti. 'I'm not to be intimidated by nasty people like you,' I told them. My therapist told me to stand up for myself and say that in any personal-threatening situation. I've been practising, so I'm good at it now. Even if I really wanted to have a widdle. 'Besides, I sent it to Mr Morton's insurance company.'

They claimed there was no way of validating the film of the incident... date, place, honesty of the film-taker. 'And you? What were your motives in filming the incident?'

'MiaLuce Tesore? That's a very foreign name, isn't it? We'll check you out. Got papers, have you? Here illegally?'

It was really rather scary, 'Here.' I copied it all onto a One Gb chip and gave it to them. 'Now do go away – *Va via.*' I pointed to the door. Rather pointedly. My therapist says I should always take command if I feel I'm being unduly pressured.

They weren't in a listening mood or mode, and weren't actually saying much at all apart from threats. 'As well as considering you for prosecution, Mizz Tesore,' they told me before they left, 'we are also looking into charging Mr Morton for malicious and vexatious claims regarding an incident on the public highway. His insurance company's records are also being studied in this regard.'

They definitely had something on their "to-do" menu. But what was I going to do? *Nothing.* All they'd done was demand the chip, although they weren't entitled to it. Nobody was, but they'd all got copies of it now. 'Let'em fight it out,' I told my budgies.

After a couple of gins, they agreed. I should be clear here: it was *me* who had the gins, not Peter, Paul and Mary – although I do let them have a sip of anything if they come and land on my hand when I'm having the occasional drink. I say occasional, but it's more like... never mind...

**

Mr Morton rang again sometime later, 'Just to let you know, MiaLuce, my insurance has paid out. It's enough to replace my Renault estate, but I'm still chalked off about it all.'

Good – that was it. Nasty-tasting episode – *Finito. Tutto finito.*

34

**

Except. The police were at my front door the following Monday. They wanted the original chip out my dash cam, and didn't believe that it hadn't been returned to me yet. They arrested me, started searching my home and charged me with obstruction. *Che cavoli!* What the heck was going on?'

Lord that was a night. I'm twenty-four. A woman – No – I'm a lady, *una signora.* My therapist told me to always remember that and model myself on someone I admire – so I think of myself as Lady Gaga-Astor. I weigh nine stone, *per l'amor di Dio*, and I'm as British as any of that lot. And evidently a total danger to society.

I could not believe it: they grilled me – well, everything but the grill. One of them kept hitting me with a piece of padded piping. Another put some tape over my mouth and nose, and something stinging in my eyes. It was like Guantanamo Bay. This is England? It was Planet Maniac Torture, more like. They don't do this in England. Asking me stupid questions about who I worked for. Oh, yes, they squirted water up my nose, too. That was horrible.

I would have admitted anything, but I didn't know anything. Then, what one said, was, 'Our officer—' and stopped short.

Ahh – that explained it all. *The midnight blue driver's a police officer, is he? Must be fairly high up for them to make all this fuss covering for him.* But I said nothing: they weren't going to get nice if they realised that I'd cottoned on. *What was he? Top secret? Drunk, or drugged up?*

I did nothing, said nothing. I couldn't do anything except let them get on with it. I was kicked out next morning, after a stern warning by a Very Senior Police

Officer in a posh uniform with a rather showy gold fishtail braid pattern. *Che vanità.*

My therapist said I should always think of something derogatory about an adversary – it takes them down in your estimation. I usually think of them sitting on the *gabinetto.*

**

I had to drop out of a couple of contracts in the next weeks – I could barely move, I was so stiffened-up. Their duffing-up lost me a few thou-quids worth of consultations. *Accidenti!*

What was I going to do about it? Like what? It was the police doing it. I reckon it was them who followed me sometimes. So I went for a nice long drive to my Aunty Violetta on Violet Hill in Mansfield and called in the garage, the estate agent, Farmfoods, and Dave's Chippy; and had a long chat in each. 'That'll give them something to think about,' I had a teeny smile.

**

The original chip turned up in the post. According to the envelope, it had been to Namibia and Australia. What the hell for? But there was scribble in blue crayon and pencil all over it – four separate lots – customs stamps front and back.

As well as the returns letter from the insurance, there was a note inside. Somebody had checked the contents, more than once.

The chip was blank – reformatted. No reason for the insurance to have done that. But someone had.

**

Then. I had another visit a few days later. It was ridiculous. Talk about K and J – a Twosome in Black. Tall man in silvered sunglasses, black coat and trousers, black shoes. And a woman with him dressed the same –

36

older than me. Both polite, formal, and insistent. They wanted in. They showed me an overly ornate ID of some kind with a phone number to ring if in doubt. 'Oh yes right,' I sniffed. 'Five minutes on Google and FakeID4Me and I could make up a card like that myself – better, probably. It proves nothing – *niente*.'

But in they came and we had a coffee. 'Decaff,' they wanted. 'Sign this.'

'And this is?' I lifted the blank sheet they'd passed to me – blank apart from a coffee ring where I'd just put her cup down.

'The Official Secrets Act.'

'Official what? Why?' I thought they'd say something like, 'Or we'll shoot you if you don't.'

And they did. They actually said it! Sweety-face had a gun. It looked very real when she showed me. With a long tube on the end. 'That's a silencer, is it?' I asked her, hoping she didn't realise I'd just wet myself. She pointed it straight at me. Oops, another dribble. So I believed them. But I still asked, 'Why?' and, 'What's this all about?'

'Keep it calm,' my therapist often says, so I made like I was in a practise session and did my breathing.

With the typical TV over-patience and tolerance of a twin *stronzino*, they looked at each other, 'Just sign it, and we will tell you as much as we are allowed.'

It wasn't that I was scared – I *was* scared, but that wasn't why I signed. "MiaLuce Tesore", a bit wobbly, 'Well, the signature box is too small,' I told them. It seemed the quickest way to calm them down. 'So what is all this about? Something to do with the car accident I witnessed?'

Sure enough, their visit had nothing to do with the little traffic bump. Not directly. 'You'll not be able to check this yourself, of course, Miz Tesore, but your dash cam film revealed two persons of interest in another car that you were driving behind a few moments earlier.'

Like a rehearsed double-act, they were. 'One is wanted in connection with funding a terrorist organisation.'

'...accompanied by someone who is known to us in a different capacity.'

'No, we can *not* say who; no names. Do not ask.'

'Thanks to your film Miz Tesore, we have identified and traced these two persons. We now have proof that they know each other.'

'We expect to make arrests in the next few days.' They almost smiled; almost smugly.

'You signed the Official Secrets Act just now, did you not? Thus, you will not speak a single word of this to anyone, *ever*. You know nothing. You have no proof, no copies, no knowledge.' They both smirked behind their mirror glasses. They probably thought it made them look more menacing. It did. I thought of them sitting on the toilet.

'No, you don't have any proof, Miz Tesore. We, er, *checked* all your electronic devices immediately we found out about this.'

'And have very thoroughly searched the whole of your home and your work area.'

I wonder if you know about scheduled posts on Facebook and Twitter? Especially mine. Not only to be posted in the middle of the night or the next day – they can be the middle of next month, too. 'And all this police hassle I keep getting?' I don't know how I had the nerve to ask.

'Nothing to do with us. Entirely separate. We imagine they're covering for a drunken police officer, that's all. Nothing.

'Not dashing to catch up with your two persons of interest, then?'

They actually glanced at each other when I said that. I think they did, anyway. It's difficult to tell when they're wearing such silly Princess Anne-style sunglasses, and I'm concentrating on controlling my bladder.

'No,' Big Mirror-face guy said, 'that's all. A senior police officer. Drunk at the wheel.'

'We have no real knowledge of that, however.'

'And even less interest.'

I was getting cross at them, 'That's all, you tell me? They battered me tit to toes, and you call it *Nothing*? I'm a revous nerk just thinking about it.'

'Indeed, Miz Tesore. Nothing. *Niente*, as you say. You have signed The Act. Be very sure you remember that.'

The woman was quite sweet after that, and we chatted. She had another decaff. I had a pinot grigio and said it was tonic. She was older than me; and she looked it. She was probably trained to be sweet and distracting while Mr Sunglasses went through my home. Again, by the sound of it.

'But how did you get on to all this?' I topped up my, er, tonic – *sai cosa intendo.*

'I must remind you about The Act...'

'Yes yes yes. I'm fed up with your Bloody Act already.'

She considered, glanced enviously at my tonic, and murmured, 'A young police officer was concerned about the actions of her colleagues in the drink-driving coverup

39

matter. She looked through the three-minute sequences on your camera chip – ninety minutes-worth.

'You're a careful and considerate driver, Miz Tesore. You leave a good safety gap in front of you, and, six minutes before the incident, you let a Mercedes in from a side street? You recall? It gave a perfect profile of two people we are investigating. The young officer is keen to advance in her career, and is very well acquainted with photographs of a great many of our Wanteds. She recognised both persons in the vehicle. Moments later, you let in the unfortunate Renault that was rammed, and we thus lost close sight of the Mercedes.

'The lady officer got in touch with us about her suspicions. We have been investigating since.'

'Er,' they asided to me, 'as a courtesy, we have performed a small return service for the police informant. It might be of interest to you, also.'

'However, you will *never* speak of this.' They departed unsmilingly. 'You signed The Act, remember?'

'Stuff The Act,' Pussy Willikins and my budgies agreed, ten minutes later.

Don't be silly – Pussy Willikins is my beautiful cat.

**

The midday news today revealed that, 'A much-sought terrorist has been taken by security officers in a dawn raid. In what is believed to be a linked undertaking, a well-known banker thought to be connected with the funding of terrorism has also been taken by security forces…' and on it went. I bet it was the two men in the Mercedes, though I hadn't looked at my sneaky copies of the footage yet: *they* might be hacking me.

I don't know about either of them – they both looked foreign and dodgy on the photos they showed on the telly.

Then! *My* Senior Police Officer was on! 'Also on this news, the arrest has been announced of the most senior police officer in...' He was mine! My nasty driver in the big blue thing. '...believed to be a range of charges including bribery, sexual harassment, perversion of the course of justice...'

'Wow! They got him!' I cuddled Pussy Willikins, 'this calls for a Gallo Thunderbird.'

Then on the six o'clock news. 'In a bad day for the police, there are reports coming in of vicious attacks on four members of the police force. All reports speak of severe beatings by four-strong groups of masked men. Two are believed to have involved violent invasions into their homes, and two were car-jackings whilst on duty. It is thought that the officers are known to each other, and work closely with the senior officer who was arrested earlier today. No senior officer has been available to comment on possible motives for these assaults, nor the extent of the officers' injuries.'

'Time I got the black Sambuca out,' I told Wussy Pillikins.

**

This evening, I was really torn about watching the footage to see if I remembered anything about the Mercedes. It's on the spare chip I sellotaped inside the little drum of food for my tropical fish. I checked – it's still there. But I *didn't* look at it, in case I'm being bugged with tiny cameras somewhere. I'd look round very carefully if I dared, but then they'd know I was on to them. Maybe MI5 would be back, or the Counter Terrorism Unit. Or Mossad, or the Feds for all I know. Maybe they all take it in turns to raid? Or launch mass joint operations through the front and back doors at the same time with those silly door-smashers like fire extinguishers with handles.

'I definitely never looked at the earlier clips.' I keep saying that aloud, in case they're listening. 'I positively don't know who was in the Mercedes.' My therapist says I should always be positive like that.

'*Dio!*' I'm getting paranoid... Will they find my secret chip? I'm all of a shake at the thought. 'Where did I leave that glass?' Peter, Paul and Mary didn't know, but we drank to it, anyway.

**

Oh, Lord, I'm *sacco di nervi* already, without this latest thing. It *can't* have been me who uploaded the three-minute clip of the nasty policeman onto YouTube's Dash Cam Network, can it? I mean, I signed The Act. Didn't I?'

But there's been a car outside all evening. I don't like to look in case they think I'm spying on them. It could be the police – I'm probably not their favourite little lady at the moment. And the Couple in Black didn't strike me as being the understanding sort, either.

However, my therapist always says I should do what I feel is right, and be positive, positive, positive about everything. So I imagine they've come to tell me they have a vacancy for a slightly tipsy nervous wreck. In the meantime, 'I need another grappa. One for you, Pissy Wullikins?'

A NEAR MISS

Yes! It's so exciting – starting my new job tomorrow. 'I'm *so* lucky,' I told mum and dad, 'against all those others. Some really smart clever girls there, and a couple of men, too.'

'But it was you they offered the job to, Maisie.'

'You beat them all, and it's only five minutes from home.'

'I can easily walk that far, even if we've still got snow. My new boss is really nice; he's got a lovely smile.'

There'd been so much to think about and make certain I was ready. I was sure I was all set, everything sorted and straight before I go to work tomorrow. Lord, I'd never settle if I stayed in this afternoon. Just silly stuff on the telly. 'I need to clear my mind. So I'll take the terriers for a long walk over the fields. It should be all clean and bright on the hill with this fresh overnight snow.'

Poop bags, two fluorescent balls, pocketful of treats – all in my belt pouch. I really needed to clear my head of everything else and get focused on tomorrow. Wow! Me! In *that* job! Jazzy and Jemima loved this walk, and would love it more in snow. Their antics would take my mind off all the buzz about the job. Must remember to say, 'Yes, Mr. *Robertson*,' not, 'Mr. Roberts.'

It's only two minutes' walk down the back lane. They know the route really well – two or three times every week we go this way. Snuffling into the snow for hidden treasures. Excited, but waiting for me obediently at the bottom of the embankment. Then I give them the wave to dash up there and wait by the roadside – they have better road sense than most people – sitting there with tails wagging like steam paddles.

I must remember to take my I.D. My passport will be fine for one. There's a bend in the dual carriageway here, rising up Beacon Hill to the left, It looks so nice here, the trees and the fields the far side all snow-covered, but the road's clear; just wet. We wait a moment to reinforce the idea of waiting. *And the statement from the bank will be alright for the other.* The signpost marks it as a public footpath just here. There's a dashed line across the road. Nothing coming. I warned Jazzy and Jemmy to go slowly and wait in the middle and they scampered across to the protection area in the centre.

Mustn't forget to make my sandwiches tonight. I followed them, and a car came past behind me just as I reached the central waiting area. They drive so fast along here. *And remember the orange juice in the outside fridge.* The footpath restarts at the other side, where it's usually a bit muddy because people trample impatiently waiting for the traffic. It'll be worse today. *Must leave my wellies out in case there's more snow tomorrow.* It's a bit awkward because the traffic comes down the hill on the long curve even faster than it goes up, and there's the slip road into the estate a hundred yards further on.

Oh yes… and set my alarm for six o'clock. Nothing coming. We all dashed across the other carriageway.

Yugmutts! That was close! Only just missed – I had to leap – Some maniac coming down the hill like a rocket, with those circles on the front, an Audi. My dad always says they're worse than BMW drivers. 'Effing lunatics,' he calls them.

I felt its draught right behind me. Inches! 'Where the Ming did he come from?' Damn – my heart was thumping as I got to the edge of the road where the dogs waited, impatient to carry on. I'd dropped one of the balls and Jazzy was champing on it in anticipation of me taking it back and throwing it for them to chase…

I waved them on down the wooden steps through the overgrowing shrubs down the embankment. Only a dozen steps this side of the road, and the usual litter was buried by a great drift of snow today. *The wind last night, I expect.* Through the kissing gate, hanging off its sole-remaining hinge, and into the field.

The official footpath hugs the hedgerow closely to the left, but that's the long way round and I want to head straight across, up the slope, heading for the old oak tree. You can see the top of it peeking over the slope of the hill, right over the far corner of the field. That's where the stile is into the next field. So we set off across the field, up the gentle, rounded slope through the deep grass. The terriers know we always go that way and chased ahead, turning to see if I had thrown the balls for them yet.

The meadow grass is deep, but it's buried under the snow today. The dogs are dashing after a rabbit or something, leaving irregular tracks through the white surface. *They'll be soaked and needing a good towelling when we get back. My socks feel soddened, and my feet are cold… Wow, that car had been so close to hitting me…*

All the way up the slope, I'm still shaking a bit with reaction to it, and feel more tired than usual. *Yes, it had been a near miss.* I'll pause for a moment to catch my breath. So tired today…

Looking back down the way we'd come, the snow looks slightly silvery, with darkened tracks and scuffs where the dogs had been circling round and chasing each other, and a rabbit they'd spotted. Their tracks came erratically all the way up from the steps and the shrubbery by the kissing gate.

Right down there, where we'd dashed across the road, a white car is parked near the footpath crossing. A minibus has pulled up. A bunch of people are on the carriageway, crowding round something…

There's a blue light flashing down there…

I can hear a siren getting closer…

I just noticed…

My own footsteps coming up across the snowy field… they should be a straighter line than the dogs' tracks…

But there aren't any at all.

MARATHON

'Do you have to work so hard at being pathetic, girl?'

'Stop damn whingeing.'

'Get over it – there'll be another race next year.'

'If you last that long with your attitude.'

Pack of cackling idiots.

'It's who *dares* who wins, not who chickens out.'

They really do think they are so funny.

'Come on, old girl… Grasp the nettle… and make a cup of tea with it, huh?'

'Stiff upper lip, My Dear. That's what you Brits say, ain't it?'

Old Girl? Fruggerty, I loathe this lot. They must Google quaint English speech and practise it for use on me.

'Man up. You're in the Good Old US of A now, Limey.'

Which was really stupid of them. I wasn't being pathetic. I was merely telling them how really childish *they* were; not me.

I did dare to win. I did. Grasp a what? I'm allergic to any kind of stings that have histamine in them, so that's off, too. Besides, I drink coffee, not tea; especially not weird sorts like these Planks have. I refuse to think of them as Yanks – Lord! they're thick as two short ones.

'Stiff upper what?' That was Hal Davey from Advertising, saying it at the top of his braying voice, 'Stiff up her… *lip.*'

Typical of that crude toe-rag, and not worth responding to.

Man up? What's that supposed to mean? I'm a girl, 23, single, five-foot tall and a really pert pair of boobs. I have "manned up", ridiculous as that stupid statement is. Why not "be a woman"?

Their idea of being a woman is lying flat on her back staring at bedroom ceilings, according to the half-arses I work with.

I have to fight my way along the Thin Red Line every morning and night; and round the office every day and I don't stand for anything. I have to be like that, because I get picked on; they are so dirty-minded and hands-on; and half of them are married. Ha! If their wives knew – probably the Stepford Bunch.

We design traffic systems, develop them, and often manage them afterwards – at least until the teething problems are over. Of course, all the men think they're the only ones who can drive – even though I thrashed them in the Team Day we had at the Indy Track. Claim women have no real road sense... unaware of what's happening around them. *Oh, yes, and who did you rear-end last week, Bubba? and who got ticketed for jumping a red light yesterday, Mr Vishinski?*

This latest episode all started because I was in the marathon, which I didn't want to do, but they made me feel obliged, said it was part of the firm's team-building program. I used to be good at Ravensdale College. We had the all-England cross-country champion there a couple of years before me. It was kind-of encouraged after him. So I thought *I won't let them down,* and I did some training and hoped my colleagues would shut up moaning about a lack of team spirit.

I'm off to a great start – all downhill at first, then a bit uppy-downy till Weaver Street, and I'm doing okay even half way round, along Wellesley and there's the steep downhill with another water point at the bottom. Some of our crew were there and they said I ought to slow down.

'I'm fine.' I said, 'getting into my stride.'

Mr Klein was there. He said, 'No. I don't care how you feel. But the CEO is three minutes behind you, and he's a regular runner. He would *not* like to be beaten – especially not by a slippy little girl. So slow right down. Limp or something.'

I thought what the hell, and I carried on. Then Jeeks from the MO comes running alongside me – he shouldn't do that, he's not in the race, and he's saying, 'You lose the race. Or you lose the job. Your choice, *Limey bitch.*' He couldn't keep up long enough for me to answer.

I got to thinking. *How much do I want the job? Yeah, it's a good job, apart from the "office banter" from the rapist clique – i.e., nearly all the men, though half of them are under me after my last promotion.*

And I was pondering it over, *How much pride have I got? Do I actually want to beat anybody at all? I don't even want to be in the tooting race, for Yoga's sake.*

So I slowed down, and I was letting more and more of them come past me, and I kept looking round for Mr Stanford, the CEO, but he was nowhere, so I stopped at a water point near the fire station and pretended to re-lace my runners. Then massage my calves, like I had cramp. Practically walked up Heartbreak and past the college. There was still no sign of him and I'd seen a dozen of our firm come past me by then and I thought, *They're all beating him,* so I ran along with Tubbsy from

49

Accounts and he didn't know anything about Mr Stanford. 'I thought he'd intended to only run the first k. As a token?'

So I'm really pissed then.

Oh, yes. This is going to be a really great place to work in future. This little farce gives me permission – absolute carte blanche – to get my own back as vindictively as I feel like. I'm frigging good at doing that – you haven't met brothers like I had. They were the most relentless pack of piss-takers and practical jokers that was ever under one roof.

So I learned from them, and became better at it than they were.

They always knew it must have been me when something happened to them, but it was a kind of game, and they never beat me up or became too violent – apart from the broken arm that Christmas. But I got Jimmy back for that; he couldn't walk for two months.

They'd either give it a rest for a time, or get straight back at me. Jake, Jack, Jim and Joe could never let it rest for long, though, so there was never much of a respite – always on the lookout.

I learned so much, how to be *totally* devious. I became so clever, gained so much experience.

In my revenge now, nothing will point at me. *Oh yes, they will regret this Marathon farce a thousand times over* – with Little Miss Sweetness being so filled with sympathy.

'Vengeance shall be mine. Starting with, let's see... bromine in the water cooler where the braying clique collect. JJ's road re-design for the Frimmingham shopping complex developed a rather sweet closed-circuit one-way system, from which, of course, there was no way out. A virus in the advertising computers saw us pushing our expertise in Boston, England; plus South Africa and a few other places called Boston. There are 36 of them, worldwide. The virus is set to change to a different one every ten days. We even had an enquiry from Boston, Uzbekistan.

The bomb threats for the firm's parking lot were traced to Mickey Mahon, 'It's his Irish background, I suppose,' I confided to the Feds, 'Old habits and all that, you know.' Stalker threats against me and Sarah M'butu were found to emanate from Al Packer's home computer… FBI interest in Mr Klein was upped when he appeared to be trafficking young boys across the state border into New Hampshire.

A kipper at the back of Bubba's top drawer gave rise to his new nickname. A fake meeting was called in Des Moines for Joey Delkes to attend – he'll enjoy the drive. Two of the section chiefs are getting all fired-up over non-existent but very plausible customers' exploratory enquiries – so much work was needed to prepare for them.

Oh, yes; there's a whole wealth of joy looming before me with these creeps. They don't come half-way up to the challenge my brothers were.

AUDREY HEPBURN
NEVER DID THAT

'Ahh, she's there again.' Same time on the way to work, same set of traffic lights at the Broadway Crossing. Me in the slow lane, she in the fast – passenger side. Almost close enough to reach out and touch.

By chance, I caught her eye, and broke into a sudden, surprised smile. She mouthed, 'Yesterday,' and I nodded back, laughing.

Long, slender neck, such a smooth complexion and big eyes; very striking. An older man driving. He glanced across, and glowered at me, and she pursed her lips, as though blowing a kiss. 'Wow!' I told them at work, 'That is my fillip for the day. Quite buoyed me up, it has.'

So disappointing. She wasn't there the next two days. I had to laugh when I got in work, 'I virtually expected her; like she's missed an appointment.' She wasn't along that section of road on the Friday, either.

Then, the following Tuesday, there she was again. Except she was driving, and he was in the passenger seat. 'He's trying to come between us,' I told my swaying hula girl.

'It sounds like you rather resent him,' my secretary said, having a bit of a smirk at my expense.

So, at Anthea's suggestion, I tried driving in the right lane, thinking of following them, but I needed to turn off before they did.

'Okay,' Anthea suggested, 'Stick your phone number in the windows; *I'd* notice, alright.'

I did, A4 size. Both sides of the car. 'She didn't notice,' I moaned. 'Yoiks – she is so gorgeous – amazing looks – neck like a giraffe and eyes like oases.'

'That doesn't conjure up quite the right picture, Skyne. She obviously doesn't fancy you, hmm?' Why do I employ a brutal PA? 'Can't you trace the car's registration?'

Apparently not; legally, and I don't know any illegal bods who might know, so that was a blind alley.

'Why do you want to know? What are you figuring on? You fancy her that much?'

'I've no idea,' I had to confess. I shrugged in rarely-felt helplessness, 'I just want to find out. I know it's silly; I don't do that sort of thing.'

'Not with me you don't,' Anthea warned. But that was a jest – she's twice my age and has four grown children.

'She's like a vision. A wondrous face framed in a car's side-window. Like some 50's film star.'

Frustrating or what? I didn't see her all through the week. I tried the same time, and ten mins earlier or later.

'Stop fiddling with that, Mr Trent, you're having withdrawal symptoms. Didn't she turn up again?'

'I can do without my secretary removing the Michael,' I told her. 'Desist.'

'Well,' she defended herself, 'it's silly—'

'I told *you* that, a fortnight ago. What the hell else have I got to be interested in these days? Apart,' I stopped her, 'from work.' I resolved to bury myself in the mundane routine of labour.

But that was never going to work, not with me. So, twenty minutes later, I decided to be proactive. The Internet – Google, Zabasearch and Pipl; Facebook,

LinkedIn, Yahoo. Back and forth from one to another to another for days on end. I even stood next to the light at the Broadway junction until a police woman moved me on; tight little bangle-hat gleaming at me.

One morning, it occurred to me, the car exhaust had been emitting vapour – which meant it hadn't warmed up. 'So she's from a couple of miles away, at most,' Pedals Pete in Transport told me.

On Google Maps, that narrowed it down a bit, 'Maximum a hundred thousand people,' Miss Walters in Accounts told me. 'But two thirds of them would probably not take this route into town: there are more direct ways for them. And half will be men; half must be children or considerably older.'

I went through census results... election registrations... Four days with many odd moments at work when ideas popped up, chasing them up at break or lunch... and pursuing them in the evenings.

'It's hardly The Magnificent Obsession,' my sister Louisa-Jane mocked.

I looked that up, 'I'm not Rock Hudson, and the lady in the car isn't Jane Wyman. But she has that film-star look about her, no mistake.'

In the next couple of weeks, I learned so much about the area to the north-east – phone codes, email addresses, street addresses, origins, children in school... Not a whisper. The car registration and its origin... sales of that make, that age, dealers. Her description... I sought similar possible images on the net. The nearest I got was Audrey Hepburn. 'Ah, that's a coincidence – the same birthday as you,' Louisa-Jane noted. 'Fifty years earlier, though. She could be our gran.'

The driver in the car? I ran descriptions of him and possible images. Got nowhere. Jack Squit.

If it was anybody else in that area, I could have found out everything. Not these two.

So I joined the flexi-time skivers, and attempted to trace my vehicular pinup's origin. I stood on three major junctions in the early morning, to see where they joined High Road – never saw a sausage, no sign of them. Couldn't even narrow it down to the direction of an outlying village, much less an estate or side street. Then stood on the next three corners, a day at a time, the same as before. Same result, too. Weirder – I saw the Merc, same model and colour, make a right turn at the second set of lights, but waiting down there for the next three mornings, there was no sign of it again.

'It's incredibly frustrating – it shouldn't happen like this,' I was chuntering to Anthea, who'd given up listening unless it was directly work-related.

But she'd mentioned it to our mutual friend, Marie-Helene, and she happened to wander along and see me one afternoon. 'I was wondering what you'd been so ratty about. You haven't bought me breakfast for ages. Or an afternoon coffee. I miss our empty chattering.'

'Thanks,' I said, not impressed with her motives.

Mmm,' she helped herself to my coffee, 'sounds like they sometimes appear alongside you on that one stretch of the High Road – between Faraday North and Newton?'

'Er, yes, I suppose so. So?'

'Aliens – obviously. And no trace of a background? There, that settles it.' Marie-Helene was quietly triumphant – as they frequently are in Advertising and Fraud.

'Believe me – aliens would set up a realistic hint at a personal history on the net. Anyway, they'd have a DeLorean, and get noticed when they merged in the traffic from nowhere.'

So I discounted that theory.

The car was there again the following Monday, I caught up with it on the inside lane, moving a bit faster than the outside lane. Yes! She was there, in the passenger seat, long sleek neck and big innocent eyes, looking as though she expected me to be there. Yes, so much like Audrey Hepburn – those delicate features, flawless complexion. 'I'm in love,' I told the swaying hula girl on the dash ledge next to the cell cradle. I stared, and almost rear-ended the van in front of me. It made her laugh and I felt suddenly embarrassed that we almost had a relationship and I was the silly end of it.

'Wow. She has this awesome smile and laugh… her eyes sparkle—' Anthea walked out my office, shaking her head. I couldn't help it – my mind was in a right tangle all that day at work, and in the evening. So I'm looking at pics of Audrey Hepburn on the net; loads of them. The resemblance was uncanny, though the comparisons weren't too equal – one in a car, half a dozen fleeting times. And the other on tiny versions of the Big Silver Screen. 'Oh, bugger, that'll be Marie-Helene at the door. She said she'd come round.'

Slightly miffed, I went to see.

'You.' God, I felt so daft saying that, and just standing there. Staring at *her*.

She held a card, a calling card… business card, as though she'd followed it for my address.

'Audrey?' I vacant-mouthed. The car was there. The man was getting out, looking angry, but saying nothing. She was dressed in a sheer midnight-blue dress, off one shoulder, a diamond-clustered band diagonal. You just do not see sights like that down Hastings Close. Not sober, anyway.

'You know who I am.' Awesome smile. *She's here, in the real.* 'May I come in?'

I must have stepped aside; she was easing past me. I closed the door.

'I have traced you at last, Mr Trent.'

'Eh? *You've* traced *me?*'

'Oh yes. You are Skyne Trent, aren't you?' It was a fait accompli, not a question. 'Did you never wonder about a name like that?' It was a challenge more than a question.

What's it got to do with you? My name? 'I know about it: they found me in the bulrushes in the river, the Trent, near Gunthorpe Bridge. Should have called me Moses, I suppose.'

That raised a fleeting frown of impatience, 'Your first name, *Skyne.* Not Trent.'

'My mum was watching Sky News? and there wasn't room to write it all on the form? There was a Post-It note stuck on my Babygro? Something like that.' She had this supremely patient smile. I gave in, 'How on Earth would I know? They just said it was. My birth certificate says so.' *Damnit… Why would anybody rake all this up?* I *never* thought about it, except when I was awake… or dreaming, maybe.

She looked different now. A touch ominous – how come a totally famous film star from before I was born was here? Audrey Hepburn never looked like this in her movies. 'We put you here. You're a sleeper. You're not responding.'

'A sleeper what? I'm not a sleeper. I never get a decent night's kip. *Jeeps!* – if you do that again, you'll see that I *am* responding. Hey! Hey! Pack that in—'

'Come…' She was slipping slender fingers round my tie, silkily undoing the knot. 'We need to communicate.'

58

'Hey. Hey... there's communicating and there's comm— Jeeps... I mean, I really wish you wouldn't do tha—'

This was ridiculous. My shirt was off, and she was pressing my hands to the silver zip down the front of her top. Impossible. I can't do that. Not with Audrey Hepburn. Or a total one hundred percent lookalike, anyway. Audrey Hepburn never did anything like that... not in the films, anyway.

'I'm due at work in ten minutes.'

'Silly. You don't do nights, not at work, anyway. Come, do I have to do all the work?'

'Yes... Er, can we take this a tad slower, hmm? What's going on?' I know I shouldn't ask, I mean, some utterly gorgeous lady is undressing me and I'm asking what this's all about? Gift horse, mouth and stupid sprang to mind.

'My daughter is to become Serenity Highness of Thon. She has no idea who her father is; and nor did I. Until I commissioned the research. And discovered you – Our lost sleeper. You are her father – in the past and in the future.'

With her single-mindedness and dexterity, I only had my pants left on. 'It is essential that I become pregnant now. So that Erye Oone be born at the correct, determined time. She must be conceived now. In this cycle. All is right for now.'

'I'm not sure I understa—'

She held my pants up. Lord, that smile – so wondrously sweet. 'We tested the DNA. You are the only possible match. You are her father. Ergo, we must mate in order to create her. *Now*.'

'Ergo? Mate?' I have never argued in a situation like this before. Face it – I've never been in a situation like

59

this before. 'What the chuff are you on about? Oh no! Really, Audrey. Don't do *that*. The bedroom? it's through there... Lord above...'

Under her spell, and tight grip round my sphericals, I followed her to my bedroom. 'Where are you from? When are you from?' It sounded stupid even then.

'Please. Hush. I *need* you to mate with me now. In this fertility cycle. You should have awakened when we kept meeting side by side along the road.'

'You might regard it as opening one eye?' I couldn't even crack on that I was awake and playing hard to get. I was most definitely hard to get. She could tell that straight off. So... I... er...

God! She was divine; such a beautiful body. Unimaginably awesome; and I knew...

I was in a dream-swim. I don't recall work or eating or anything except her. There must have been, I suppose. 'No-one ever had a body of such perfection,' I worshipped at her navel, and above, below and beyond. *It must be me going mad, or drugged, illusioning... imagining.*

The films I'd been watching her in, these past few weeks – with Tony Curtis and Rock Hudson. And she's here in my house, my bed, looking so much like she did in the film Tiffaney's... My Fair Lady. Yoiks to the moon and back – she was My Fair Lady, alright.

One week later, it was over. She went out and didn't come back. Her absence somehow felt so final. I knew it was over. Like a dream and I was waking up. But it hadn't been a dream – Anthea at work had seen us out at the Mexican Sonora Restaurant. She commiserated when I confessed that I was alone again.

The next morning, the car was there again. It slowed down in the outside lane. I looked, knowing.

I was wrong – a cascade of near-white blonde hair with wild curls and a huge smile. Caught my eye and waved, long fingers wriggling. An overdone pout.

Jeez... I was into full staring mode again. All the pipping and blaring behind me woke me back to reality.

She was in the Merc three mornings that week, as if she was sizing me up. No uncertainty this time, not like Audrey.

I checked on ImageMe and Zapa; Piple and WhosTheFace.Com. 'Marilyn Bloody Monroe?' That was the nearest I could find. 'Very much the same,' I kept murmuring with each image I studied. I printed a photo off and stuck it on the backseat window. Along with turning the dashcam to face sideways.

'Yes, it's her. Same bright smile; or it's some future alien modelling herself, or *itself*, on Marilyn Monroe. Or her film image, anyway. Beaming when she saw the photo, and blowing me a huge, exaggerated kiss. Same driver – completely ignoring both of us.

She was at my home that evening, posing there when I opened the front door. She must have been practising – it was the exact pose from some movie or other; I'd watched half a dozen in the past two or three days.

Wow! Posing there, 'You are something else,' I told her.

Her opening line was, 'Some like it hot. *Do you?'*

On past form, I knew this wasn't going to last, and it hardly seemed worth wasting time and mental effort on asking what her cover story was, but I did.

It was the same as Audrey's: she needed a child by me, to be conceived in the very near future – some temporal something had glitched. It was beyond her, and

I wasn't all that concerned after the first breakfast together. She admitted her name wasn't really Marilyn. 'You couldn't pronounce the real me.' I tried, but it was like the most convoluted one you've ever heard from Eastern Europe, multiplied with three degrees of complexity.

'You're right,' I agreed, 'Marilyn.'

'We consider you to be remarkably valuable, genetically. Exactly what I need in my son. So… if you'd be so kind?'

I was resigned to her loss seven days later, having done my best by her.

'So that's another week of your life wasted,' Anthea consoled me.

'Personally, "wasted" is not a word I would choose.'

'Think there'll be another?'

'No idea. She didn't say anything beyond her own situation.'

'Perhaps you should look over a few more movies from the 60's and 70's?'

The 60's and 70's? The car alongside me had this face from heaven. Maybe literally, for all I knew of their origins. Not a face I could place – very pretty, long mass of solid blonde hair… *No – not a face I recognise.*

I was into the 40's before I matched her on Google – Veronica Lake – starred in a film called The Blue Dahlia. I felt like a paedo when we met up: late teen, five feet-three tall and a complexion out the nursery… Awesome lady.

Sophia Loren lasted longer than I did. The contrast with the previous week's sylph-like lady could not have been greater, physically. Six inches taller, and at least as much again on the bust measurement. She was more than a handful in all kinds of ways...

'Honestly, Anthea, it's one after another. They're divine. I'm in Hogs' Heaven. Any red-blooded feller—'

'Or randy git, as we call your sort where I come from.'

'Course I am. What am I supposed to do? Offered on a plate, or a bed, or a chandelier, if I had one. I got to make the most of it – accept my fate, as it were – while it lasts.'

An awesome lady called Greta Garbo had an accent and sultry drawl to die for – I almost did – I very nearly walked under a bus when I was thinking about her one morning, in a state of near-exhaustion.

Hedy Lamarr was brighter than anyone I ever met before, as well as gorgeous and imaginative...

Doris Day... *Impossible,* I thought. *I can't, not with Doris Day.* But she could, and we did...

'The Mercedes was on the High Road again this morning, Anthea.'

'Oh? Recognise your latest alien bedmate?' Anthea was getting jealous, I reckoned.

'Well, definitely someone I recognised. I know the face, but the name escapes me...'

I pondered it again. 'No. No good. It'll come to me. I'll get on Google tonight.''

'Looking straight at you? Eye contact? What did they look like? Hair style, colour? Glasses? No idea which films they might have been in? You must know – you've been surfing the movies from the past hundred years.'

'Oh, you'd know… entertainer… really flamboyant pianist.'

Andrea puzzled for a moment, 'Pianist? Always a bit showy? Not Hélène Argerich?'

'No, no. Spectacular performer.'

'Erm… Khatia… thingy?

'No; never heard of her. Really over-the-top glitzy pianist entertainer…'

'The only other one I know is… whassername? Libby Schuman.'

'That's it!' I remembered. 'Libby—'

'Libby Schuman?'

'No. *Liberace.*'

'*Liberace?* Wasn't he the er…?'

'Yes.'

'Oh, dear, Mr Trent; I wonder what his cover story's going to be.'

'Never mind Liberace. I'm more worried about who they might have lined up for next week.'

BUSTER

'Don't look at me, Dog Breath, I'm a cat girl.' I stared at
this ragged-haired mongrel in the porta-cage on the
passenger seat. 'You're surplus to requirements – and
surplus to the age limit, too. So stop looking at me in that
tone of voice.' I knew what the policy at the RSPCA was
– three days' bed and board, and if unclaimed, put down.
Kinder this way – on him and my nerves.

'Nothing I can do for you, Buster. You're a stray.'
He'd been running wild round the neighbourhood since
Higgins my next-door neighbour had cleared off. Good
riddance to him, lecherous old hairy-nose. His scruffy
fleabag of a dog had been barking and crapping
everywhere, especially at me and in my garden.

'Cats don't do that kind of thing,' I informed it, for
the last time. Supposedly gone into a nursing home, old
Higgins, near his kids in Sussex. 'Probably buggered off
with that grey-curled old girl he keeps meeting down the
Dog and Duck. You been deserted, old spud—'

Smat! Fraggle! Slammed. Smashed. Massive crash.
Rammed sideways. Car's rolling over. Grinding shrieking
noise flooding me.

Crashing down an embankment through trees, rolling
twice – at least, bursting open. I'm trapped in it. Creaking
and hissing on its side. I'm hanging by the seatbelt.
Shook up to Bodmin and back, I'm trying to undo it.
Corn Cobs! It's fraggling difficult. Hanging there… soon
as I undo it, I'm falling into the bottom side – sprawled

feet in the air against the passenger window – which is smashed and got twigs and grassy stuff coming in.

Could hardly think, or move – so ignominious, upside down in my own car – what's left of it. Wrecked. At least I don't have a skirt on, showing my drawers. So fast. Must have been hit by something big. Sideways. Helluva struggle to even think, much less twist over. *Dog's gone. Cage, too.*

Get oriented – car's on its side. Manage to stand and look out the smashed side window. Feels like it was my head that bashed it in. Don't half hurt down my ear. All down that side, actually. Footballs! – I hurt every-bloody-where. My specs gone, too.

Peering out the window, facing the tree-tops. *Frags! I'm miles off the road,* and really struggling to heave myself out and sit on the door. *Nobody else round. But there had been other cars.* Yoh – so dizzy! Waited a mo to let my head settle and feel my tender bits, feet dangling inside the car.

So what do I do now? Look again – do I clamber down the underneath where it's all filthy, oily and hot exhaust? Or slide carefully down the roof. You don't think of these things until you're in the situation.

Well, *I* don't.

So I started to slide down the roof— Shit!! Tore my knee on something. Caught my trouser leg. Pulled and heaved and jerked to get it free. Corn co—! the car was deciding it needed one more turn, overbalancing with my weight. Came rolling with me. I squawked. Too late. It was on me, rolling belly up – or wheels-up.

66

Phut phut phut! It's on top of me, crushing me, a bit of a wobbling rock as it settled, and I'm bottom-half under it. Can't breathe, hardly – more like bottom two-thirds trapped. Can't crawl. I'm smelling petrol, smoke. And something's sticking into me; very painful.

Can't shout. No breath. *Just wait. Think. I've been rammed off the road. Hit by a lorry? Saw it out the corner of my eye, did I? Did I see another car get swiped, too?* Can't think. Or move.

Just wait. Somebody'll come.

They'll come…

Soon…

 Two people have come down. I can hear them talking. They're peering into the car from the other side. Saying, 'There's no-one. Must have been thrown clear.'

'Or climbed out.'

They're leaving…

Quiet.

The bloody dog was there, tail wagging. The damn thing knew it was free. Inches from my face. Gloating at me. It barked. Backed off when I pulled a face at it.

'Oh footballs; I'm stuck.' Too crushed to breathe right. Can taste blood. Not enough chest movement to call out; no breath…

Just wait, Dais. Just wait.

Tasting so much blood in my throat. Frags. So stupid to pow out like this. *Ufff… Shuggerit, it's pressing on me more, settling. Phutting Toyota.* It creaked – moved a fraction. It's phutting heavy. It's gonna roll more... its balance starting to go...

The dog's back, sneering, 'I told you so. On the other foot now, eh?' It sat, smug. Looked at me, wagging its tongue and tail.

'You needn't expect me to beg,' I told it. 'You scruffy mongrel. Funny how things change round, eh? Me on the block now.' I coughed. More blood. *Strong* taste. *Feel it bubbling in my chest.*

It barked, right in my face. 'Shiitake mushrooms! Don't do that, Buster. Clear off, Dog Breath. Make your bid for freedom' It barked again, inches away, gloating at its new-found freedom.

Not long now. My brothers might be a bit upset for a time, but I've left my house to them, so they'll get over it soon enough.

 'Someone's here.'

'In this one. Trapped underneath.'

'A woman.'

Voices shouting further away; then calling closer; down near me, speaking. Police-sounding. Vaguely seeing a face. Young woman, scrubbed clean, cap falling off as she peered at me. Hands reaching at me. Tried to reach back. Hands won't move. Two people touching at me, shaking heads. 'You awake? Alive?'

Damn dog barking again, right in my face. *God, dog, your breath.* 'Push off, hound.'

'She's alive. Get the medics down here; the rescue crew. Get this car stable. Branch or something under here.'

68

My breath came in shallow rasps and blood-tasting spittle… fading light. Can hear screams as they're lifting the car off me. It's me fraggling hurting everywhere and I'm sure I'm going to burst out in blood all over the place once it's off me – like the car's a massive pressure bandage keeping all my blood inside.

Air bags either side of me inflating. Car's rising. I'm being dragged out on something. Stretcher. Doc-type peering and pulling faces and poking. 'Need to get her in quick. You know your blood type?'

He mean me? 'O Neg.'

Being lifted and thumped and bumped up the embankment. Back of an ambulance. Laid out. Drips everywhere. Two other casualties sitting whinging in there already, somewhere past my head. Two sticking drips and things in me. *Saline,* I'm thinking. Somebody's talking to me about a lorry driver… hit four cars. Brakes, or drunk, don't know. 'You're getting the best attention… what's your name?'

'Dais… Dai…' Might be some morphine, too – the screaming's died down. *Bet I'm bleeding like a halal calf…* new blood pumping round my legs where they were flattened.

'Both legs. Multiple fractures. Pelvis crushed,' I'm hearing. Then I'm not.

'Daisy? Daisy? Miss Field? Are you awake? Coming round? You're in hospital. ICU.'

Some gruesome blurred nurse. Male. God. Has he been mauling round me? Another one. Doc. Senior nurse. 'You've been in an induced coma.'

'For nine days.'

'But you're recovering now.'

They're a bit nervy. Edgy. 'So what's the bad news?' *Shit. I bet I lost my legs.*

'We had to amputate your legs. Both of them.'

'Above the knee.'

Poo on a shoe! I knew it.

I was listening. I didn't hear much. *Both legs gone. I'll cry tonight when I'm on my own. Lord, my heart's thumping, somewhere low down in me, where it just sunk.* I reached down the bed. Yes, I ended there. Ached. They're watching me. For my reaction. *You don't get to see inside me. I'll cry tonight. Till then. I stay on top.*

'My brothers been? Any visitors?'

'You've been in a coma.'

'So nobody bothered?' *Typical. I'll change my will.*

'A young police lady came several times.'

'She your friend?'

Bar steward – a male nurse sounding pejorative. I've got a few put-downs up my sleeve for you, if I need them, Bug Face.

'Yes. Very much so,' I said, just to chalk him off. 'She coming again? Tonight? You don't know? No? Okay.' *She'll be the one with the unsecure hat.*

It was. She called in that evening, visiting time. That was the most awkward I ever felt. Thanking her for being there – sounds so stupid. For helping. Being in the ambulance.

'I wasn't.'

'Oh. Wonder who was, then?'

She did have a really nice smile, like quizzical sad for me. I can do without that. 'They have your dog at the RSPCA.'

'Dog? No, I don't own a dog. Oh, that one? What did he do? Come barking to you? Lead you to me? He needn't think I'm beholden to him.'

'No. He didn't do anything like that. He was just there. Thought he was with you. He isn't yours?'

'No.' *Filthy creature. Huh – it didn't even bother to go fetch help. Nothing to do with me. I was only getting rid of it. Clearing the neighbourhood of all its disgusting little packages fouling the pavements.*

She chatted, PC Windsor... Victoria. She didn't have to come to see me. *Maybe I'm her project; or her first near-fatal RTI.*

Whatever the reason, I wasn't about to ask her – I was having enough bother staying together. But I liked her. Well-scrubbed pink face, even at the end of the day. Looking so fresh. Smart. *I never look that good after a day's work. Never will again. Work's gone. Tennis... I'll be in a wheelchair. I'm brimming up. I'm fraggled if I'll cry in front of anybody. I don't lose control. Ever.*

'Not your dog, then?' she said.

'Buster?' *Scruffy thing. Foul breath. Didn't even have the sense to alert anybody. Just... just stayed with me. Close, rubbing his nose in my face, licking me. I remember thinking, crushed under there, If I die here, you're my only companion; my last-ever company, you tatty little mutt.* 'What about him? He's at the RSPCA, you say?'

'Yes,' she brightened up. '*Do* you own him?'

71

My first tears trickling, 'Actually, I think he owns me.'

THE CAUSEWAY

'It'll be alright. Fine.' My dad was laughing and really sure about it. 'They're always exaggerating these things, so there isn't a rush for everybody to get off the island all at once. There's plenty of time before the tide comes up that far. And it won't be getting dark just yet.'

'You're always right, Dad,' I told him. 'They *are* a load of daft ap'orths, aren't they?' He always called everybody that when he didn't agree with them.

'That's my girl.'

He looked at mum, but she didn't say anything. Like she usually doesn't when Dad's being "himself". So I said, 'The last time to be off was more than an hour ago Dad. Are you sure we'll be alright? And it *is* getting dark now.'

'Don't you start,' he laughed. I wish he wouldn't always laugh at me like that. 'It was an hour and a half ago, actually, but the wind's against the rising tide, so it holds it back, slows it down at least an hour. And they always give at least half an hour extra, just to be safe. So we're fine.'

It only took us five minutes to drive from our cottage to the start of the Causeway, 'There. See? You can't even see the sea.'

We looked out the car windows and he was right: all we could see was mud and bits of seaweed; but there wasn't much light over that way, anyway, so we couldn't see much of anything. 'See over there?' Dad said, 'That's thrift growing: it sure doesn't grow underwater. The tide

73

doesn't come up this high. Not as high as the causeway road. They just like to scare folk.'

The road was fine and dry for a whole long straight part and the sea was miles away across the dead-flat smooth sand. Then it went in a big curve left and there were big dry sand dunes sometimes. Then we went through a wet patch and there was spray all round the car from the wheels and Dad was laughing because it was like fountains on both sides. A car coming the other way was flashing its lights and Dad said, 'That's because he can't see through all his own spray.'

Me and Jimmy were in the back and the seat's quite low, so I undid my seatbelt so I could stand up and see it properly. And Dad said, 'This's pretty exciting and special, eh?' Mum wasn't saying anything.

I could hardly see where the road was because the wet was all over, 'It's only like rain's made puddles on it,' Dad said. 'We can always see where the road is because of the sand heaps on each side, like little dunes where they've cleared the wind-blown sand off the road sometimes.'

'And there's the little white posts with the red reflective mirrors on them,' I could see them on both sides of the roadway, so it was alright.

We went up a bit of a bump in the road and the road was dry again and my dad was laughing that there was no bother... 'Ay up, here's another wet patch. See ahead there?' We went down a little bit and into the water again and there was spray all round us in front as well and I couldn't see anything much but Dad could – he had his wipers on. I couldn't even see the red reflectors on their little posts, and there weren't any sandy heaps and clumps of grass but Dad knew the way and Dad's always right. But I was in the back with Jimmy, anyway and we couldn't see as well as Dad could.

Mum was saying, 'We ought to go back, I'm worried, Max. It *is* getting dark.'

'Don't be stupid, Diana. It's only another hundred yards ahead till we're off the Causeway. See? That's the far side, where the gate is, with the two watch-towers... That's the Tollgate Inn just beyond. Oops...'

The car was going down a slope again and I could see the water in front of us was darker and that meant it was deeper, 'Max. Don't drive into...'

'Do be quiet, Diana. I'm concentrating. Just have to navigate this last bit.'

The water *was* deep. It felt like the car ran into it and slowed right down. There was all this water sloshing round the sides of our car, and some of it splashed right up onto the bonnet.

'It's okay... okay... nearly there.' Dad knew what he was doing.

I couldn't see anything, and there were no lights to see and Mum was crying and Dad told her to shut up, and it was getting slow. Then Dad said he couldn't make it go faster and it was stopping and some water splashed up on the bonnet again and my dad said it was stupid and he was getting cross with the car not starting again. And then the car started wobbling all over the place and I sat back down and held on. Then the car sort of went sideways a bit and was like shaking and jumping and the water was all coming up on Dad's side – right onto the windows in big splashes, and it was all swirling on my side. Dad said, 'The stupid engine isn't doing anything at all now,' and he was shouting at it. And the lights went out, inside and outside. It seemed everso dark then.

Mum said, 'So what do we do now, Max?' She was really cross, and said it wasn't the poor car that was stupid.

That started them rowing, and I said, 'There's water coming inside, my feet are splashing in it, Mum. Should we be getting out?' And I was trying to reach Jimmy's seat belt and Dad turned and said he'd belt me if I so much as touched it. And I said, 'He's only three years old, Dad, and he can't undo it himself.'

A wave bumped into the side of the car as Dad was turning round to me and he smacked me across my face and said, 'Well, just get out then, little Miss Knowall,' and he tried to drag me close to him and he really frightened me, as well as hurt me. And there was more water round my feet and the car was going sideways again in little jumps. 'Go on, get out if you feel like that.' He sounded really nasty at me and I wanted to get Jimmy undone but Dad stopped me again and I was mad at him and I kept back from him.

I had a real fight to get the door open and it suddenly like sucked me out and I tried to climb on the car but it was all slippy and the water was cold and all waves knocking and pushing at me so hard, and I couldn't keep hold of anything and I was gone from the car. It was even darker then and I couldn't see it.

I didn't hear Mum and Dad's voices. I splashed so they could see me, and so I could get back but I seemed to be moving quickly in the water and it was cold then; and I was all on my own and in the dark. It was more scaring than anything that ever happened before. And I was sort of crying because I was on my own with just water all round, but I did swimming in school and with Mum and Dad and I knew how to just lie still and float on my back and save my strength. So I was trying to do that with just my face out the water, but I was getting water coming over my face and it was really salty. But I kept as still as I could and knew Daddy would come and find me.

But it was ages and ages and I was like crying to myself and really frightened more and more, and it was totally dark with no lights at all. And cold. I was all on my own with nobody with me. Or to help me. And it was getting worse and I was being spinned round and it was so very black. All on my own. The water was becoming lumpy, with swirls and waves and I was really scared and wanted to cry and shout. But there was nobody there, so I was going to keep saving my strength – Daddy always said I talked and shouted with so much energy it was a wonder I wasn't exhausted all the time. I couldn't tell how far away it was back to our car. So I just sort of waited and got colder and colder and tried not to swallow any more water. But it was sploshing in my mouth with the little waves and it was horrible and salty.

I got sure I was going to die. But Mummy and Dad always said we had to be brave, whatever was happening. 'Being brave is what saves people,' Dad said. So I tried to be.

Then one time I thought I heard voices. It was after a long long time. I tried to shout and wave but I couldn't do either and I was splashing, and swallowing more water and it tasted even worse and I kept feeling sick and I was getting really really frightened then and I'd been trying to stay everso calm and brave till then and now I was so scared and on my own and frightened... and I was thinking I would be drowned and nobody would ever find me if I just sank and went to the bottom and was washed miles and miles away and the fish and things would eat me. They eat your eyes first.

I was so tired then and I heard the voices again. But they were in my head like daddy miles and miles away.

I thought my clothes were too heavy and making me tired but I couldn't try to get them off because my head went under the water even more and making me not breathe. And it would make me colder and I didn't want to not have any clothes on and anybody find me like that. And I was really frightened and really tired and like crying but not crying.

I was blinded – a big flash suddenly... black again and I was going mad I was crying again I was going to drown and never be found and what would my mum and dad say? I bet they'd cry.

It was all bright and blinding me and noise roaring all round me and a monster had got me and dragging me up to its lair or its nest or something. I was crying more and shouting and trying to knock it away off me but it was lifting me up and up into bright blinding light and dropping me hard on something hard and there were lights all on me blinding me and monsters shouting and making noises all round.

I was crying and couldn't stop shaking. And the monsters had bright glaring lights and were wrapping me up in their great horrible webs to eat me later and saying things like 'Got her,' and 'Found her,' and 'Thank God,' and 'Get on the phone' and gripping me tight like they were never going to let me go.

'I want my Daddy...'

And the monsters all went quiet.

CINDA
WAS IN ONE OF HER MOODS

'Now you just listen to me, you hog-face redneck, there is no way in God's Little Acre that me and my wife are gonna drink a bottle of Red Hole Moonlight just to suit an inbred shitbrain like you.'

'Harold, don't antag—'

'It's alright, Lucinda; they need telling straight.'

It wasn't the best continuation to an evening at the Atlanta Road House Bar, but they'd been asking for it, and wouldn't let him alone and he was only minding his own business and, 'I'll drink to who I want and not who a horde of drunken goober-grabbers order me to drink to and I don't care what you're celebrating in your stupid baseball. Damn rounders, yer like a pack o' girls. So some pea-brain got a rounder. Big deal.'

He absolutely knew it wouldn't go down well, but he didn't care tuppence. Nothing had gone down well for the previous half-hour when he was being amazingly reasonable in his super-pleasant conversation with them. 'So I come in here for a quiet drink with my wife, and get picked on by you pack of drunken imbeciles—' He knew it was unwise to call them that, but expected it would merely speed up the inevitable; they were hellbent on persecuting somebody and if it was gonna be him, then his wife wouldn't be included – he'd focus them on himself. 'So stuff yourselves back down the hillbilly drain you crawled out of. Leave me alone or I'll show

81

you how a real man can take care of himself, especially against a slurp of noodle-brains like you glassy-eyed toads.'

Like he cared, anyway, as the big loke laid hands on his shoulders to pull him up from his half-eaten trout pomegranate and fries. 'Aw, shuggs, you loog-brain,' he twisted out the hulk's grip, and launched himself at the twisty-mouthed moron who'd been leading the victimisers since they swaggered in and laid their eyes on the couple in the corner.

Might as well lay you out first, Harold decided, in his usual frame of mind, and his fists rammed and jabbed into the face of the tormenting bully who was a foot taller than he was, surrounded by two-dozen equally pin-minded creatures from the black lagoon – which, as he suggested, was probably just outside o' town.

Winning, he was, with the lumberjack-shaped lummox flat on his back and floundering, lips split, nose the same and yelling in a panicking, utter-shocked series of yelps.

That was when the trouble escalated. It had started as one local bully picking on a tourist couple passing through – trying to intimidate the Limey into drinking the valley's homebrew; and mock-mauling the guy's wife. Then he was threatening them both, pouring drink over them. Harold was *so* restrained – she'd warned him before they even entered the place. But the altercation was clearly leading straight to the fight which Harold was obviously winning – when eight of the other brain-donors decided to help Ugly Joe by dragging Runty Limey Shite off him and beating the crap out of him. It wasn't entirely going their way: his renewed retaliation sent them staggering back in the face of his yelling and fist-flying counter-attack.

The mass-brawl gravitated towards the swing doors, driving its unruly way past the leathers-and-studs brigade of Bikers rowdying, drinking and joshing among themselves, all grinning broadly, watching with mild disinterest as some out-of-towner who should'a known better took a kicking and hammering from the local 'dozers. The loss of a few of their drinks, jostling their arms, and kicking their floor-boarded helmets didn't endear the Pick-on crowd to them, but they weren't in the interfering groove tonight.

Besides, the event was scrapping its rowdy way outside, onto the darkened, fairy-lighted veranda. So all was well in the world of Harleys and Indians, with a couple of Crockers and a Bonnie thrown in... Or, actually, it was Harold who was thrown in. Headfirst down the front steps in a tumbling heap. Landing in a sprawling, bloodied, heap across one of their bikes – a Springfield Thunderstroke.

Instant rage, indignance and retaliation mode came over the nearest dozen Bikers as the bike collapsed under his sudden impacting weight, knocked into another – a 57 Harley – and he bounced sideways into one of the Indians, which dropped crunchingly on top of him, struggling to rid himself of the offending heap of metal.

Red rags and a field of bulls had nothing on this. Three Bikers rose as one, and stalked down the steps, terminal violence in their eyes and clawed fists. Cursing in deathly mutters at the creature that had defiled their gods – two lifting the Indian 78 off the thrashing loser.

'What the hell you done? What the hell's a con rod doing here?' Another wrenching at the fighting-back heap... 'What the hell's this? Y' damn leg? Where's y' damn leg? Legs – y' got prossies?'

'Makes no never mind. Rip'em off him. Gerrim up.' Hands jerking and ripping, pulling him upright.

'You got no legs, y' stupid shite?'

Bloodied and still ragingly determined, Harold fought to be free and get back up the steps to the local dullards, but The Bikers were bigger and more numerous than he was, jerking him from one to another, pulled back and forth, shirt tearing open... laughing in total power over the defiantly snarling English idiot.

'Leave him, you pack of thugs,' Five-foot-three, Lucinda was all fight, scratch, and fists..

'Wha's this?' A couple of mouths and grasping paws rounded on her.

'Get yer greasy hands off us, you pack of girl-assed faggots.' Harold's right fist handed out a blinding black eye to The Biker who was mauling at his wife's chest.

'Get off him, or I'll rip yer eyes out,' Cinda was in one of her moods but, in truth, it didn't take a lot of effort on the part of Six-eight Lex to hold her back, telling her to calm it and 'don't wanna harm you, lil lady'.

'America Home of the Brave,' another one proclaimed, jerking at the broad ribbon round Harold's neck, repeating the words as he pulled the ribbon straight, 'and what's this? Yer keys? Hey, we got us a Toyota Pickup. You're going for a ride, *Harold.*'

Held and punched, hands grasped and searched at him... ID tags... A badge. 'What the fuck?' Passing his things around, laughing in anticipation of the fun at hand.

'The 21st? What you doing with tags from the 21st?' The question was punch-tuated with a fist.

'Buddy swap...' Cinda snarled at them. 'Get off him.'

'Buddy swap? This miniature creep?' The derision was dripping. 'Like from where? Who with? Buddy with the Honey Puppy, are you?'

'Mind your own. Get your maulers off me.'

'Iraq, two years ago,' Cinda was spilling the beans. 'Bezier Camp. He was on attachment with the 4th.'

'That right? So how'd you get this?' A new great hairy face demanded, clutching at the tin badge...

'Mind to yer own business... it's mine.'

'He was forward observer with the Yanks.'

'Lucinda!' Blood trickling from lips and one cheek, Harold was furious. 'Don't tell'em anything. None of their business.'

By then, half the inner bar population was out on the veranda gawping and cheering The Bikers, all sneakily grateful it wasn't them who'd been picked on – it didn't take much some nights. And the locals only liked to pick on little guys who were new in town, especially foreigners, particularly Brits.

'Just a minute. You got no legs. I heard of some guy out there got his legs blowed off. What's your name?'

'Mind your own... uff!' Knowing he was deep in it didn't make a scrap of difference to Harold. It wasn't how he did things. Not ever. Lashing out in rage...

another fist into a gloating face, the satisfying splatter of blood. *These guys never learn to keep up their guard.*

'Hammer him,' a shout from the gallery. A row of lit-up faces along the veranda rail.

The Biker with the wiped-off grin rammed him back in the face, and Harold was returning to the dirt of the parking lot, pinned down and helpless to do anything more than writhe and curse.

Lucinda was fighting, dishevelled, horrified, 'Leave him... leave him...' Only little, but The Bikers had a kind of respect for the sanctity of decent women, as they saw it, though not their own women, or any they regarded as whores. So Cinda was getting better respect from them than she had from the inbred yokes...

'Wasis name? *Harold,* did you call him? Wimpy name for wuffs, Harold.'

'It's Viking. Means Ruler of the Army. So you get some respect in your thick heads or I'll—' The rest was lost in the laughter. Cindi's mood worsened.

'I heard of a guy out there, a Limey. Always ordering everybody round. The other Limeys loved him. Wasis name...?'

'Marsh. Harold Marsh. Sergeant with the British forces. Never talks about it.'

'So how'd he lose his legs? What's with the Buddy swap – how come he's got US tags?'

'Don't tell'em, Lucinda – nothing to do with them.' Harold fought to get the boots off his chest.

'Gerrim up...'

Lucinda was pulling her light jacket off, rolling her sleeves up in a ritual display. 'He was in Air Strike Coordination. Forward observer with the Yanks.'

'At Bezier, huh? My brother was there... said about some Limey who got it. Legs gone. Must'a been you?'

'Nothing to do with you. Get off me or I'll have your balls for earrings.'

'Dragging two of our injured guys back. Went back for the third. Didn't make it all the way back with the third one. Mortar got'em. That you?'

'Him?' The incredulity was plastered everywhere, every face. *'Him?'*

'Let's see the tag... and the other. Shit, Mack Duran. He was Andy's buddy. Made it back together, they did... don't know the other guy.'

'Let him up,' The Biker's tone was changing, 'Get him right.'

Hoisted to his feet – sprung teronite feet – Harold's rage was equally focused on The Bikers and the cat-calling local horde up on the veranda. But he paused for a moment – *Lull them, Get your breath back. Let'em think you're done. Then launch at the biggest guy in the middle.*

But The Bikers had more sense and kept tight hold of him, still cleaning him down, seeing if he could take a batting down their style.

'Come on. Inside. Have a drink with us. We'll get you cleaned up. You too, little lady.'

'That was you, was it? Dragged two of our guys out? Sorry about the treatment. This lot,' he waved dismissively at the local crowd. 'Don't worry about them.

The scrucky'un who was hitting on ya, he's the sheriff's son. Likes to throw his weight round. We can sort him, quiet-like, y'know. Won't be any more bother from him.'

With little choice once his rage began to dissipate, Harold allowed himself to be escorted back up the ignominious steps to join Cinda and the Three-three Brigade in a few drinks and dark looks across to the quietened inner-bar drinkers and diners. 'Hell, no more trouble, *Harold*, huh?'

He quelled himself. Harked back to the advice from doctors, therapists and his wife – *"Get yourself under control, Harold, or the rage rules you."* He knew it, and had learned well – from necessity. 'Okay,' he sat with them. *"Take responsibility. It's not always someone else's fault."*

Besides, if I don't exercise some self-control, Cindi'll only get in one of her moods, and wallop me; or stick my legs in the freezer again.

'Just one of them things,' he said, trying to defuse down. 'I know I'm not easy when it comes to bother… ask Lucinda.' *Just make sure you ask her nicely – she's working up to get moody.*

They waved for drinks, brushed him down a bit more, gave the sheriff's son dark and threatening looks, and asked, 'So how come you went and pulled three of our guys out of harm's way in Bezier? It was you, was it?'

'Yes, that was me,' he confessed, and half laughed, fingered at his drink. 'We were in a forward foxhole, observing, calling strikes in. Got targeted with mortars. Took one close and we was ordered to get out of there. We got two dead, and three with mod-severe injuries –

88

gut, legs, head. Not mobile. I was okay. I had to get'em back.'

He laughed, a half-laugh, 'Hell, no way I was leaving them there.

'They were shit poker players. I pulled'em out in the order of how much they owed me from the night before.'

COLD NIGHTS IN CANADA

It was a coach tour of Western Canada, centred on Alberta – Calgary, Edmonton, Lake Louise... About forty of us on the tour, all Brits, I think. Billed as the Northern Lights Tour.

'That's the highlight of the ten days,' Max the guide said. 'We have two nights far out in the wilderness north of Fort McMurray. Absolutely black, unpolluted skies, so we get the best possible views of the aurora.'

But there was loads of other scenery and places of interest as well. Every day.

We had this fat little feller on the tour. Lived in Birmingham, I think, from the accent. Bromsgrove, perhaps. And, wherever we were, he'd always clamber off the bus and decide he'd prefer to go in the café rather than walk two hundred yards to the viewpoint. Or along the trail. Or down to the lake-shore. 'Or wherever,' he said. 'I don't do scenery and suchlike.'

Yeuk – that accent!

Asking him about not going to look at the latest scenic marvel, he'd say, 'If the mountain will not come to Mohammed, then Mohammed is damned if he'll go to the mountain.' And he'd retire to the nearest gift shop.

Or he'd come out with something like, 'If Mohammed was meant to walk distances, God would have given him a motor.' And he'd park himself with a hot dog and litre-size coke.

His other one was, 'God gave Mohammed a large stomach in order for Mohammed to show his appreciation, not to starve himself.' And he'd head for the nearest diner, while everyone else went to see the eight-hundred-foot waterfall.

'But you're not Mohammed,' I'd say. 'You're Hector Higgins from West Bromwich.'

'And you're an atheist,' his wife poked him, in our support.

'You're just fat,' his son confirmed.

'And bone idle,' concluded his daughter.

'I'm still not going up that sodding mountain,' was always Hector's retort when looking at the footpath through the forest. Or the ramp up to the cable-car. Or steps into the hotel. Or even onto the bus on one occasion.

Thus, every time we arrived anywhere, Mohammed Hector stayed put in the café, with sufficient double Americanos and chocolate cookies to feed his family as well as himself. And he contentedly slurped the next few hours away.

Even when we went out one night after supper, he was no better. We drove right into the wilderness in the coach to see the Northern Lights. We were twenty miles from the nearest man-made lights. Totally black sky where we stopped in a hunting lodge for a few hours. It was remarkably warm and comfortable, with loads of nuts and trail mix with chocolate buttons; plus hot cocoa.

'Okay, Hector,' I challenged him. 'So it's cold out there and a foot of snow in the car park. But for Heaven's sake, you come four and a half thousand miles, on a tour called "The Northern Loights"' – he only understood it if you pronounced it like that – 'and you're gonna stay indoors and not even bother to step outside for foive minutes to look at the Aurora?'

'If God meant Mohammed to freeze to death he'd have made me an eskimo. Oroight, Dene?' And he went up for his third mug of cocoa and another handful of M&Ms.

It was catching – not a word of a lie – we were the only ones who saw anything. Jo and I went outside in the car park. Complete blackness in this clearing in the forest from about 11.00 p.m. onwards, and we waited to see the sky's display.

All the others either got fed up waiting after ten minutes, or stayed in the warmth round the iron stoves. At midnight, the heavens started to light up. The spectacle became more and more intense, and spread across the entire sky.

Even when the lights were in their most awesome display, the only ones out there were Big Max, our Driver Guide, and me and Jo. That breath-taking glory overhead, above us and around us; flickering green curtains that drifted and draped on every side; purple-tinged… with touches of orange… a sort of electric tingling in the air. Absolutely phenomenal.

Big Max gaped up at it as much as we did, 'It's the finest display I've ever seen – greens… Those shades of purple… yellowy oranges. Incredible.'

Out the goodness of my heart, I went inside the lodge to tell the rest of the group – sacrificing five minutes of that glory. But not one of the lazy sods would stir themselves away from their cocoa and get their noses out the trough. 'Too cold out there, Dene,' they whinged. *All converted to Bromsgrovism, huh?*

'If God wanted Mohammed to look at the skoi, he'd bring it down here for him to see properly.'

'Okay, fine, but me and Jo got heaps of the most amazing video and photos imaginable.' A few of them had a look at some of our pics, and pulled faces and mumbled about hot chocolate and nuts.

'It beats me why God bothers with you,' I told'em over supper the next night. 'He goes to all this trouble to make the world's most amazing Whisper and Light Show, and you won't even stir yourselves to glance at it.

'Jo and I are going out tonight to see if we can spot the Perseids. You know – the meteor shower that comes round every year? It should be at its best tonight. Predicted to be exceptionally good. It'll be ideal in this pitch darkness. We're going to wander down the road about a mile; to that high knoll that overlooks the lake. The hotel's got plenty of torches to lend out. Maybe get some fabulous reflections in the lake water... the mountains the far side... some time-lapse pics... vids? Anybody fancy coming with us?'

My invitation fell on deaf ears. Not one of them.

'I don't blame them entirely, Jo – there's no guarantee that we'll see anything much; maybe a few tiny streaks high up, spread over the night. We could be hours out there with nothing to see.'

'Not everybody's cup of cocoa,' she agreed, 'staying up all night in minus ten-degree weather on the off-chance of seeing some shooting stars.'

'Yeah,' I pulled a face and accepted it. 'Can't blame them, I suppose. We're the only ones daft enough to grab a flask and a couple of torches and walk a mile or so along the lake shore and up a steep little hill – in this freezing weather.'

'Supposed to be getting warmer tomorrow,' Jo predicted.

That night, it was extremely cold, and Jo kept mumbling some John Denver song about Cold Nights in Canada. 'But there's no wind, so it doesn't feel *too* bad.' As we

94

trekked along the lakeside, the reflections in the lake were beautiful. A touch of Northern Lights reflecting delicately. It was well dark by the time we arrived at the top of the knoll. 'Good job these torches are decent.'

'And come with spare batteries.'

We set the big cameras up, and took a couple of pics of the distant hotel complex, looking warmly welcoming. 'Hope these meteors are worth seeing tonight,' I gazed at the hotel, almost wishing we were still in there in the snug comfort. Then fixed the cameras pointing east for the expected – hoped-for – arrival of any tiny streaks in the sky. Gloves on, parkas zipped up high and tight, and flasks filled with hot Bovril. 'Our illegal import,' we laughed, 'the Canadians banned it from being imported, along with Marmite!'

'Pervert colonials.'

The Perseid display started well, around eleven o'clock; three streaks appearing slightly to the north of east. They were almost together, spreading apart a little as they approached. Ten minutes later, another one kept coming, getting bigger and so close, right over us in the upper atmosphere, then carried on behind us. Awesomely bright, leaving a long vivid streak in the sky. 'Great beginning,' Jo was delighted. 'Super practice for turning the camera on its tripod to follow the movement and keep the focus right. Nice, smooth action.'

The pics were pretty good, and we'd have been more than satisfied if they were the only meteors we'd see all night. 'That was just so much brighter than any meteors I ever saw before.'

'Middle... lower atmosphere before it burned out.'

'Hey... I can see better.' The scene was a bit lighter. We looked round, expecting it to be the aurora returning.

95

'Bugger. The sun's coming at us,' It lit up the black sky.

'Straight at us.' You really do think, "Shit – this is it," and accept it. 'It's gonna happen.'

But it was deceptive. It wasn't quite directly at us. It was actually a degree or two to one side of us. Lower by the second – out of about ten seconds it was visible.

It hit. The other side of the lake. Right about where the hotel was. Huge explosion, like a thousand bombs. Such a flash. Massive blinding flash. Lit up a trail of smoke behind it.

A shockwave radiating across the lake, it would reach us... 'Coming so fast.' People say stupid things like "I was transfixed." I know exactly what they mean.

'The trees're bending this way.'

It hit us. The sheer blast – the light and heat and shock-wave.

I was smashed over, hurled back. Glimpse of Jo tumbling head over heels.

The fall backwards saved us, I think. We were in the shelter of the rocky tip of the knoll when the debris started to crash and roar all around us. I've never been so terrified; huge lumps of rock crashing all around us... Whole trees end over end... This roaring gale. Something vast hit not far away. I got hit by a few bits. Couldn't see Jo. Had to protect my head. Trying to kneel up and see her.

'Chriiiiist!!' A wave of scorching heat. Baking. Like opening an enormous oven door on five hundred and sticking yourself in it. I was roasted. Something hit me again, big, splattered me flat again and falling further down the slope.

There was this enormous glow. The whole sky was red-orange. Fire coloured and radiating.

A cowering age later, the rain of small debris tailed off, apart from one enormous thump that can't have been too far away – I felt the thump shock through the ground. I was crawling round in this red smouldering light. So weird. Calling for Jo...

Found her forty or fifty yards away, clutching at each other, 'What the hell happened?

'This's hell...'

'I'm battered everywhere,' she was almost laughing, 'bruised everywhere, too. Nothing broken, though.' She was shocked, but she's tough; wasn't histrionic about it at all.

A bit of cussing and effing and blinding, 'What happened? Isn't it obvious? One of the meteors became a meteorite – it landed.'

'Yeah, it was so huge, just a second or two.'

'Yeah, Jeez, Jo. We really witnessed it. Actually saw it hit.'

'Couldn't tell anything, though. It was all afire. It could have been the size of a house or a football stadium for all I could tell.'

'Looked like it was right near the hotel. Shall we go back up and see?'

'I can't move,' I told her. She thought I was being mardy, but I really couldn't. 'Something isn't working somewhere. Think my legs are numb... whatever.' So, after a bit more cuddling each other, she went back up the knoll to see.

She was back after twenty minutes, 'Everything's gone in that direction – just a fire blazing – half the forest as well as where it hit. Looks like there's a massive pit there. All like raging fire. And the lake's wobbling all over – waves in all directions crashing into each other. And so many trees down, even on the top of the knoll where we were… I found your camera near there… *Here.* Mine can't be far.'

I turned it over, 'Looks a bit melted. Tripod's twisted. The memory chip might be okay, though.' I could barely focus on it. I kept fumbling it; dropped it.

'And it looks like there's been a massive wave come almost all the way up the knoll. There's debris and water all up the far slope.'

'Jeez, Jo, we're bloody lucky not to have been drowned…'

'It's so hot up there, where you get the glow directly. We could have been roasted…'

'Or steam-bathed…'

'I think I have been.'

Jo was poking all over me – found the problem. I'd had a bash on the head. 'Feels like a depressed fracture, Dene. You're concussed. Lost coordination.' And my left arm was a bit mashed up. But we managed to stop the bleeding, 'Definitely broken… feels like multiple fracture. I think it *must* be blood,' Jo told me, wrapping half my shirt round my head, and the rest to strap my arm tight. 'It's hard to tell in red light.'

I needed to get back to the top of the knoll and see for myself. It was the biggest struggle I've ever had, even worse than climbing Cotopaxi. But I got there, sort of half-crawling, and half-shuffling along on my backside. Shuggs – that hurt everywhere, 'I *gotta* see,' I told her.

From the top, it was utterly mind-blowing. 'Jeez… The whole far side of the lake's glowing.' Blazing… scorching heat. 'Yes, that's *exactly* where the hotel was.'

'Nobody could have survived.'

'Not one of them.'

'You still got your pocket camera, Jo?'

She was staring at the ever-rising mass of sparking, fiery smoke, the lit-up forest and mountain sides, the shock waves still catching the light on the lake.

'You may not blame'em, Dene, but it sure looks like God did.'

'Eh?' I said, too dizzy to think.

'The meteorite *did* come to Mohammed.'

GO ROUND AGAIN

'Go round again? What do you mean? Go round again?'
Standing there on the pavement, Mum was looking very
harassed. JD, the Best Man seemed a bit fraught, too. Dad,
in the back of the super-stretch limo with me, was looking
panicky. I don't care who's supposed to be where – it's
my day and I'll go where I want, not where everybody
tells me. For once.

Even if I am in a beautiful stretchy car – like the song
says – long enough to put a bowling alley in the back. I've
done three tours of the estate already. Four would be four
too many round this estate.

I was all for leaping out and sorting somebody out by the
throat. But Mum shoved the door to again, 'Boris hasn't
turned up.'

'Boris hasn't turned up!?' I know I shriek when I'm in
that sort of temper... er, mood. 'I'll kill him. Right. Round
again. And you, Freddie Wilkins, can wipe that smirk off
your silly face, and get driving. Slowly, round the block.
Different route. And get a move on – slowly.' I gave Dad
my bouquet and waved my fist out the window, 'Five
minutes or he's dead, along with you, JD.'

'Might be ten minutes,' Freddie Wilkins said. 'The
traffic's building up along Front Street. And I wasn't
grinning, Ma'm.'

'Don't you cheek me, Freddie Wilkins. I know you.
Sitting there all posh in your dad's stretch taxi. I bet he
owes a fortune on it, doesn't he? Do something useful –
drive, before I become too irate for anyone's good. That
Boris! My Boris! My proposed hubby. Unreliable as ever,
but Mum and Dad kept pushing us together.

'Maybe he's stuck in traffic,' Dad offered.

101

'Or come to his senses.' I saw Freddie Wilkins mutter that. He was grinning in the mirror.

'Freddie Wilkins. Don't you dare speak again. Or smile. Or think anything. And don't Ma'm me again.'

'No, Ma'm… I mean, Yes, Ma'm.'

'You always were trouble, Freddie Wilkins. I remember you in school. Always up to something. What are you up to today, eh?'

The church loomed large, yet again. The gathering on the pavement was looking restless, all head-waving looking for signs of Boris and his brother. 'We've got the dogs out looking for him,' some A-hole claimed. *He'll die*, I swore, *straight after the reception.*

'Go round again. Just once more. We'll find him.'

'Round *again?* I'm heading for despair here, Mum; the sandwiches'll get stale if we don't hurry. It's the last time,' I warned them. 'I'm sick of the scenery round there – and people are noticing – there's a group next to the post-box cheering me past every time. Alright.

'You heard. Drive on, my man. Clock it round the block. And you stop your grinning. Or else.' That Freddie Wilkins always needed keeping in his place – too snappy by half, he was. 'And you, Dad, stop wittering. This's the last time.'

Back down Front Street, I was furious. My Day! Rapidly heading for being ruined by Bothersome Boris. 'And you're no help, Dad. You're supposed to get these things right – Yes, alright, the Best Man, too. And you're definitely no help, Freddie Wilkins. Keep your eyes on the road. I remember you, alright – always hanging round with that gormless girl, what did you call her?

'Sis. She's my sister, Freda. She's had the operation now, and she's not like that anymore. It was a brain tumour pressing—'

'Alright. I don't want the full cut and slash commentary, thank you. Just look where you're driving.'

'Yes, Ma'm.'

'You're grinning again, Freddie Wilkins! Just don't dare, not in my presence.'

We did that circuit in record time – I'd had more than enough, besides, I bet somebody would be at the sandwiches if we were much longer. They were clustering on the edge of the pavement, all looking a bit anxious now – not as fraught as me

'Ah, they're waving us down. Pull in, Driver.'

'Yes, Ma'm.'

'Grrr – you call me that once more, Freddie Wilkins…' I remember him well enough. He was always hovering over that ginger girl; with his head buried in books and computers. He could drive when we were in Year 8! He was 14! He used to drive round the speedway the other side of the park. And on one of them trails bikes, as well. Heather and Chloe were chasing after him, but they said he was too fast for them. It was their idea of a joke.

'There's been a message, Margaret…' JD looked kinda nervous about telling me.

'He hasn't gone and died on me, has he? I said I couldn't rely on—'

'Almost, Margaret: he's under arrest in Folkestone, with their Bertie. Trying to smuggle themselves onto a cross-Channel train.' He cringed back when I lunged at him through the open window.

'I'm not wasting all them pork pies and canapes,' I told my dad. 'You'd better get this sorted, JD, or I'll sort you.' He quivered back among the others – a few smirks there, I noticed. 'Drive round somewhere else, Freddie Wilkins. I'm not having that post-box lot betting on my time per circuit again.'

He was definitely smirking as we cruised the limo away from the kerb. Decision time. 'Freddie Wilkins! What are you doing this afternoon? This weekend? The rest of your life?' He was laughing. Not just his face – his shoulders were going for it, too. Cheeky devil: he was always laughing about something.

He was turning round, still with that big grin, 'Was that a proposal, Maggie? After all these years?'

'You keep your eyes on the road, Freddie Wilkins, not on me. There's plenty of strawberries and champagne.' Well, it was just a thought – I've seen worse than him. Maggie *Wilkins*? Hmm, that had a sort of ring to it – a wedding ring, maybe. 'So how about it, Freddie Wilkins?'

And he had the cheek to say, 'The one who's doing the proposing should be on their knees, Maggie Duffin.'

'If you think…' I wasn't having that, him and his so-called humour.

'Almost there, Madam.'

'Do not "Madam" me, Freddie Wilkins.' This was definitely desperate… He *was* funny sometimes… and not bad looking. And all the guests were gawping on the pavement, hovering like a pack of vultures. He pulled up, catching my eye in the mirror – challenging me. That did it! I climbed out. Like an avalanche I was, in that dress, and gathered it up with maximum decorum, and went round to his side. 'Dad! Lift my dress up. I'm not going to mess it up.'

I knelt there next to his posh white taxi, and I did it! I proposed to Freddie Wilkins! 'Marry me, you great grinning grasshopper. Or else.' Dad took a picture – he was my official photographer. Everybody else had their phones pointing at us and were probably beaming it live across the social universe.

Freddie climbed out. To be fair, he looked very smart in his driving suit. Probably the same one for funerals, I reckoned. He still had that cheeky grin; if he dared to turn me down, I'd have his grin on the griddle.

He abruptly stuck his hand out and helped me up, even smoothed my dress down. 'You watch where your hands are touching, Freddie Wilkins, we're not married yet.'

'Come on then, Maggie: he crooked his arm, 'the next lot'll be arriving soon. We might as well go in together now.'

'That's true enough, Freddie Wilkins, 'Nobody's coming between me and my man again, but we'll walk. I am *not* running down the aisle for anyone. Dad – you get yourself down there and tell the vicar he's got the name of the groom wrong. Here, have you got a pen? Or just remember, it's Freddie Wilkins. Go on, go tell him.'

'Can I really have champagne? My dad'll drive the stretchy. And cucumber sandwiches? And kiss the bridesmaids?'

'You're pushing your luck, Freddie Wilkins.'

Half-way down the aisle by then, I gave him my hardest look, and he came up with that cheeky grin again. 'I can see I'm going to have bother with you.'

'I was just thinking the same, Maggy Duffin.'

He stopped. On one of those faded gravestones they set into church floors to remind people about mortality – just what you need at a wedding. What was up with him? What was he going to do now? I was petrified. Shaking – all these so-called friends still scrabbling for their pews and mobile phones. Oh Lord, what now? 'This, Maggie Duffin, is the exact spot where I intended to stand and shout.'

'Shout what?' This was getting worse.

'"Now I know, I can't let Maggie go!" When the vicar got to the bit about any just cause or impediment, speak now – I was going to.'

'Going to what?'

'Speak, tell him I got a reason.' He looked at me gone out.

'And what was that? What reason?'

'I… er… I'm not saying *that* in here, Maggie…' I've never seen anyone look so shifty.

'This is the best place to say it, Freddie Wilkins, in a church. Whatever it is – you might as well tell everybody and show me up.'

He shuffled – some of'em had their phones on again – 'I was going to shout, "It's me who loves you Maggie, more than that fat toad Boris. Don't marry him; have me." Like in the song. Beautiful South.'

I was aghast. *'You weren't?'*

'I was, I wrote it down in case I got tongue-tied. Look.' He wasn't grinning now – he meant it. 'Go on then, Freddie, shout it now.'

He did. Everybody was clapping and cheering and laughing and videoing it all.

That was four years ago and we've a little girl called Eleanor – which means God is my light. And a baby boy called Emmanuel – and that means God is with us.

He must be, because we are all *so* made for each other. And some of the credit goes to his dad's stretch taxi – we put our mattress in the back, that first night. Eleanor dates from just about then.

106

CONVERSATIONS
WITH A BOTTLE

Yes, since you ask so nicely, I'm drinking whisky. Yes, again... or *still*, if you must know; haven't stopped for ages. 'I like you, don't I, little bottle?'

I often talk to the amber contents of my latest glass. Or bottle. After all, it is the essence of all understanding and benevolence. 'And you like me, don't you?' I hold it close to my eyes to stare into its all-knowing depths. 'It's mutual, isn't it? Which is more than I can say for anything or anybody else: you always make me feel good; and you never upset me, do you?'

I don't care how it comes – neat; or with dry ginger; room temp or iced – cheap supermarket blend – they're pretty good, actually – or a smoky single malt. As long as it's whisky... or whiskey from the Emerald Isle. Or Wales... Canada... Japan... You can do world tours on whisky.

'After eight months in close companionship with you, I'm used to your little ways. We won't get much chance to be together in future. So I'm making the most of you now.'

And probably spend my first six months inside drying out. 'You can anticipate fourteen years,' Mr Useless Fatpig, my solicitor, told me.

They're going to find me guilty tomorrow. "Causing death by dangerous driving whilst under the influence of alcohol... Leaving the scene of an accident..." It's all there. It's a very big book they threw at me. Fourteen years'-worth of Big Book

'I still have no idea what happened, except my car hit a boy on a bike in the road.' But I haven't drunk enough yet for the glass to start answering me. Everybody tells me they know what happened, and call me stupid and stubborn to keep insisting I wasn't guilty. 'We even have flashes of doubt ourselves, don't we, little glass? Though I can't remember if the doubts come when I'm sober or kaylied. Can you? No?' I don't get many straight answers from the glass, to be honest.

Nobody believes me. Not even my solicitor. I'm resigned to it now. The jury foreman will say, "Guilty, m'lud, on all counts." Or something like that, and the judge'll sentence me to the max – no mitigating circumstances, no remorse, no admission of guilt. 'That book they throw is going to land awful hard, eh?'

It was a Friday night after we'd been out drinking. I was the designated driver for the four of us… Julie, my wife; Alvin my neighbour; and Bernice from work. Big joint celebration: Bernice had a promotion, and Alvin had a small lottery win, and it was our anniversary – four years. 'That was before I met you, eh? My little nectared friend?' I never drank much anyway, and it was my turn on the driving rota – so I was okay with it.

I never touched a drop all evening: it would be too easy to get carried away or nobbled by some silly sod. I remember the whole evening perfectly, etched on my mind. Some of it too vividly. 'You believe me, don't you, little friend? But everyone insists I'm imagining it, deluding myself, a defence mechanism. I clearly remember the Greek restaurant in town, all the ouzo and whatever the wine was. Loud music and great food. Some dancing and more booze, but I drink the *non*-alco beer on these occasions. Always.

Then we went on to the Duck and Grouse and carried on with the party there – great time – plenty of R'n'B music and lively atmosphere. Crowded in there, as always. 'I think I need a drop more of you, little one. You pour beautifully.'

We were due back at eleven, for the babysitter, and I wanted to get a move on; we could carry on back at our place or Alvin's, and Bernice would stay over. She was on-off with Alvin, anyway, and I could have a couple of glasses.

But they were right in the mood for it then, and wanted to move on to that new club in Somerton; they were really in the mood for a knees-up. I was saying 'no' as nicely as I could. "No no no," I was insisting, "The babysitter... we promised." They were reluctant about agreeing, but did.

Then when I came out the toilet, they'd gone. So had my jacket; and my car.

I remember wandering round the pub car park, bewildered. I couldn't believe they'd done it – I'd have called them, but my phone was in my jacket, and they'd taken it. 'Choices? I ask you, divine little friend.' I had one option: to walk. It was about eight miles, and it was very dark once I was away from the lights. I got cold and lost, and slept in a bus shelter in Ulverham – the next village along.

'That police welcome was a bit of a surprise at nine in the morning when I arrived home, wasn't it?' Promptly breath tested – negative – but they were pretty nasty about that, as well as about something else... strong-arming me down on the floor, and slapping me about.

Eventually, I found out there'd been a crash – my car had hit some kid who was racing round the streets at that time of night – and, naturally, the car driver gets the blame – plus fleeing the scene of an accident. The landlord at the Duck and Grouse swore I'd been drinking, and left with the others – as if he knew – he was in the lounge bar, and he wanted to keep his licence. The Greek lot couldn't remember us from Zorba, just a heavy-drinking small party. 'One of many, eh?' *Ángloi pínoun polý,* he shrugged. That's the English for you.

"But the others – They'll tell you. They left me…"

Like hell they would. Talk about a conspiracy – according to them, I was driving and had done a runner. They all swore to it.

"*Husband* is a temporary sort of legal term; a mere word," my wife said, before starting divorce proceedings two days later, complete with custody of Janice and James.

"*Neighbour* is purely a matter of short-term geography, just a word, meaningless," said Alvin, whose lottery win was considerably bigger than he'd first admitted.

"*Friend* is a flexible concept, open to interpretation, only a word," said Bernice, and didn't seem to mind when Julie moved in with Alvin as well. Apparently, it had been their frequent custom and practice of late. My wife, for chuff's sake.

I was ordered out my own home. It was either go quietly or resort to enormous physical violence which wouldn't have made me feel any better, or solved anything.

'So I've been rotting in a grotty cheap hotel with you, my little liquid friend – my only friend – for eight months. I kept going to work, but things were getting bad there, suffering the slings and arrows and all that jazz. Mostly stirred up by Bernice, I gather. So I go less and less often – I have to report my whereabouts to the police twice a week, anyway, don't I? Jeez, you taste *good* tonight. They

110

confiscated my car and suspended my licence, so I'm going nowhere.

'So, tomorrow – it's today now – they'll find me guilty and it's down I'll go. I'm really, really scared. I'm terrified of standing in court and everybody looking at me and thinking what a bastard I am. I'm dreading the process of being taken away – the officers – the stripping me down, the transport with other prisoners, the hard guards, the cold cell. The next ten years in prison. Ten years, if I keep my nose clean, they say. My life'll be over. It already is. Reduced to a toothbrush and toothpaste in a poly bag.'

Exactly as I'd envisioned it, all through the night, I went to court in my work suit, being escorted in – two courtroom guards or custodial officers, whatever they call the thugs on duty. I took my usual place at the front. No solicitor. 'He's done a runner, too, huh? Can't face it, huh?'

The judge was becoming a mite tetchy after five minutes; and I was restless: this was putting off the inevitable. The jury members were irritated – probably had the shopping to get done whilst claiming a full day's expenses.

The judge sent someone somewhere for something... and then my solicitor came grovelling in, all huff and apologies. He leaned up against me, very theatrical, he was. 'I have some new evidence,' he whispered. 'Hold your breath and cross your fingers he'll let me introduce it at this stage.

'My Lord,' he said, 'before I summarise the case for the defence, I have one more piece of evidence to present. With your permission?' The prosecution objected and had a row about it being too late, no warning, where had we been hiding it? They did a lot of whispering at the judge's seat, and retired to a back room for eighteen minutes. Almost twenty minutes knocked off my time inside.

When they came back, it was pronounced that, in the interests of justice, the evidence could be presented in open court.

The landlord of the Duck and Grouse might not have had his CCTV switched on, but a joiner and shopfitter called Wright was there in his work van. And he had his dash cam on. It always automatically downloaded the footage to his computer. His wife had recalled they were there that night, and something had recently reminded her of us – some loudly raucous joke from Alvin, I expect. And they'd left at the same time as us.

There it was! In grey and grainy ghastly truth – my car vanishing – Alvin at the wheel. Me there a few seconds later, wandering round and pathetic. Cursing. Very much as I recalled. Stomping back and forth infuriated.

Oh boy, watching it, I was empty, dead, crying, falling. My knees had jellied. The jury watched it in silence, had a few questions from the jury room, and came back with a Not Guilty verdict; plus a recommendation that there should be an investigation into the conspiracy by perjurious witnesses to pervert the course of justice.

Three days later, I still can not believe the verdict, or what my so-called friends had done to me… my wife. I'm just as empty; just as divorced; just as friendless; still out of a job. I'm still in this tatty cheap hotel, while Alvin still lives next door with his three million quid, and Bernice; plus my wife on frequent occasions, for all I know. Actually, yes, she's my Ex-wife now. I don't feel any different. Almost disappointed not to be going to jail. Almost… there'd have been someone to talk to, at least; some routine. I've split up with my liquid friends from Scotland and Ireland, for now. And I'm utterly lost. Been missing my kids all this time. Even missing Julie. I hate the mindless telly they have in here – day and night.

Someone's at the door? How come you can tell it's the police, just from their knock?

Of course it was them, with a social worker. 'The three accomplices have been arrested and charged with conspiracy to pervert the course of justice. They will all be released on their own recognisance, pending a full hearing.'

'They are not permitted to meet each other…' The tall constable said.

'Would you be prepared to move back to your home address, and take custody of your former children? Temporary, perhaps longer term?' That was the banjo-hatted WPC.

I nearly hit her for the use of "former", but I was too busy on Cloud Nine saying, 'Yes yes yes, please yes!' My heart was suddenly flying with the skylarks and my eyes were stinging.

'And have your wife on the premises as well—'

'*Former* wife. It's her who's "former".'

'—otherwise, she would have to spend time in the cells. Tonight, and perhaps longer.'

'And then move into similar accommodation to what you have here.' Social workers always need to have their say.

Shuggeration… what the hell do I do? I hate her… Don't I? The cells'd do her good. Or living in a dump like this, on her own? Yes… Just right for her. She'd hate it, absolutely. 'Why? Why have me there?'

'We don't permit the mother to be alone with the children—'

'In case she—'

113

'Alright, I get it. Having me there'd stir her up even more. She loathes me.' Could I? Let Julie stay in the cells? They were soul-destroying; it would be awful for her. What do I do? Anything to be with James and Janice. And their mum and me? Like it used to be? Like I'd imagined it had been. Having to be civil for their sake. I wondered what poison she'd filled their minds with. Could we make up? In any degree? What kind of example would we set if we were together, back in that house? But, to have Janice and James with me again – I'd imagined they were gone forever.

'Anything. If it could help,' I said.

'There is a proviso—'

'A stipulation: a social worker would visit each day, and a WPC would spend the first night with you.' She smiled, very weakly. 'Me.'

'To assess the risk of... er, domestic trouble. Would you be able to accommodate her, with her own room?'

Oh, Lord. My mind flashed through three or four possibilities – and the only feasible one was for Little Miss Uniform to have the guest room, and me and Julie to use our own room again, together.

Or me on the settee...

I'd said, "Yes", again, before any answers and all the negatives came flooding through, but I didn't care about them. I'd be back with my children. I could put up with anything for that. I could learn to. Considering that I'd been practically suicidal last week, and even more so an hour ago, I could put up with anything.

It might not be for long, if she was found guilty, and jailed.

Or if she annoys me too much.

114

DIVERSION

I waited while some local guy finished serving himself at the gas pump. He called the cost to the old feller just coming out the tumble-down filling station – pale blue clapboarding that needed re-nailing and repainting.

They decided to chat a while in the shade of the sun veranda, one leaning on the ice-freezer, the other against the coke machine.

'Do not beep, Jeffrey Penn. We'd never get served.'

'I know.' It's how they do things: the pump-keeper serves anybody he don't know. And he takes the cash or a card first. Regulars serve themselves, pay by account.

The crusted-up old guy came over eventually, tiredly waving his customer friend away and motioning us forward.

'Full?' he said. 'Got a card? Going far?'

'Right across to Painted Springs...'

'Long way. Scrubland all the way. Remote stretch of road. Bit winding.' He came round, wiping the windscreen, kicking the tyres, peering in the back, filling her up. 'Plenty of water? Food? Cells? Charged up?'

'We're okay for everything, I think. Thanks. The road's clear enough is it? Made up all the way? Not sanded over or closed anywhere...?

'No. It's all fine. Couple of stopping places for photo-opportunities, if you want. They're signed. There's a cave with rock paintings and carvings...' He hitched his dungarees up again, and finished fuelling up the Toyota. 'Just watch out when you get there. Anybody hanging about out there ain't up to no good. Been reports of

115

muggings along the middle stretch, and at the pull-out with the climb, too. It's an old volcanic neck – the Devil's Horn, they call it. Good views of the rock tower from the road, and you can climb it for the desert views from the top. Like I say – keep an eye open for muggers, thieves and jackers. Nine dollars. That it? You or the lady need the restroom? Don't get many Australians out here.'

'Think we're okay, thanks, and we're Brits – from England.'

He looked at us with saddened eyes, I thought. 'Careful out there, then, young feller. Funny folks about. Don't stop for anybody along the road – they'll try anything, and they're up to no good.'

'Cheers. Keep the change, huh? And thanks for the info.'

'You watch it now.' He waved a wrinkled, dried hand in farewell and went back under the shade.

Cruising along, not minding the blazing heat, 'Wonderful change from England this past month,' we decided. No sign of anyone at the first pull-out, and yes, the volcanic neck was a spectacular near-black tower sticking out the pale desert sand. 'It was the pipe the magma came up and poured out the top as lava,' Lexi summarised the information board, almost unreadably bleached by the sun. 'About two hundred feet of softer surrounding rock have been eroded away, leaving this neck as a totem of Ute Nation pride – it says here.'

We walked round, but sun was too hot to try the climb up something that high and steep, so on we cruised towards the four-hours-distant motel for the night.

The cave sounded interesting, but there were people around, and Lexi pulled me back, 'Remember what the gas guy said. Nobody's up to any good out here.' So we held off, and a couple of them were edging closer to us. Another one wandering closer to the SUV.

'Right you are. Back in. No point risking it if they're as dodgy as they look.'

A bit on edge, we were glad to get back on the road without any trouble, and it was easy, comfortable going. A mostly-flat road that wound leisurely between dunes and rock outcrops, or dipped into wide, dried-out flood valleys.

Relaxing travel, the car handled well, and we'd been glad of its four-wheel ability a couple of times in the past few days, going off road to out-the-way photo opportunities. Smooth and quiet on the made-up surface, too. The scenery varied both sides – flat sand washes, bare rock platforms, dense scrubby undergrowth... cactus groves. It gets to be a monotonous, colourless backdrop after a time. There was even the traditional cow's skull with horns by the roadside, maybe parts of a backbone and ribs trailing away from it.

'Another couple of hours to the motel,' I broke the peace of the drive, 'The Mule Trail, is it called?'

'Mule something...' Lexi reached for the note she'd made when she booked it on the mobile last night. 'Oh. What's that?'

I slowed down a bit, peering ahead into the heat haze. The road kept vanishing in shifting glass reflections, shimmering upwards as the surface reflected more heat than the sand and undergrowth around here – quite dense, uneven scrub in patches. No people or ruined dwellings to be seen anywhere; too hot and barren for any kind of survival out here.

I slowed a bit more, puzzlement turning to worry as we approached. 'That something across the road? all the way across it? Hard to see for the heat haze.'

'Is that someone there?' Someone was waving, as though for help. 'Jeff, don't do it. Keep going. The old guy said…'

'I can't drive through that. It's a bloody tree – twisted oak or something. It's too big to crash through. Besides he's on his own.'

'Don't be daft, there could be others hiding anywhere. Jeff – you gotta go for it.'

'Okay, okay. I'll go round. The sides. I can drop her into four-wheel D at this speed.' And pushed the button, lifted off, and down again.

'Jeff! The bank off the side is too steep-sloping. We'd roll over!'

'There's no way I'm reversing and going back, Lex.'

Christ, my heart was thumping. And dropping. *This could be bother. Real bother. Could be bad…*

Close now. Someone else rising from behind the tree. Some guys suddenly pulling branches onto the sides of the laid road surface. *That's the side doors closed.* Less than a hundred yards away and still slowing…

'Jeff!!!! Do something!'

That galvanised me. Almost as much as the guy who was raising his hands. He's got a gun? 'Fuck!' We were in bother. Deep deep do-dos. And I had no idea what I was going to do, but my foot was down all the way and trying to get further through the floor. A puff of smoke. It *was* a bloody gun. 'Shit shit shit.'

A way out? 'Get yer head down! Lexi! Now! Right down.' Shoving at her. She was screaming. I was yelling and going for'em. The windscreen banged. Glazed over in quarter-inch cubes. I'm half crouched down clutching the wheel and still screaming at them. The screen went altogether, crashing in all round me and I was sure I felt a bullet smash past my head and hit the padding behind me. Pedal right down. Thirty yards maybe, and must have been doing seventy. Something definitely hit my shoulder. Bullet. 'Fuckit I been shot.' For a split beat, I thought about it – I'd often wondered what it would be like to be shot. *Now I know. Felt like nothing – a slap on the shoulder from a friend. Like "Wow – I've been shot.'*

Except I was high and raging-thinking. What about Lexi? What would they do to Lexi?

Everything so incredibly fast. Weird – I could have described each hundredth of a second as I was aware of it happening in every detail. No more control once I'd seen a gap in the undergrowth, sort of, and gone for it. Then it was in the hands of Him Upstairs. Big G, as Lexi says. The Toyota bounced and jumped. Crashed up and down. Off the road. Thick scrub all round.

Truly – it was way past my influence then, though I knew exactly what was happening. The Toyota careered into two guys. Splat – and Splat-thump. Faces panicked.

A gun raised. Suddenly loomed out the scrub. Weird again – I got like a photo of that gun in my mind, even now. Another grinding, crashing, bouncing moment. I'm struggling in something like a clear-minded panic jumble – the wheel leaping everywhere in my hands. Branches slashing at my face. That was blinding. Nearly crying. Felt like we were nearly vertical, crashing nose-down in the sand and scrub and bouncing high. Another branch smashing into my face. *Damnit, I won't be able to see anything if my eyes fill up with blood.*

Now I got something stuck under the wheels or axle or something... not got the power... wheels losing it... I'm jumping up and down and heaving on the wheel to make it keep going. Total panicking. 'Keep going keep going keep going... Need distance between us.'

I couldn't look round to see. Didn't dare. Be too scared if I saw them. 'Damn. Slowing fucking down.' And I'm ranting and bouncing and heaving on the wheel and we're grinding to a stop... Absolute, sheer panic. *What the fuck do I do...? What to do? Must do something. Yes. Get out. See what it is.* Dropping out. Soddit still in gear. Back in. *Soddit soddit. Into neutral.* Scrabbling round. Gunning the motor. *Feels like the right rear wheel's lost traction...* scrabbling babbling to myself... *What what what? Do something.* Could see them. Running towards us. Four... five of them?

Something caught underneath both right-side wheels? Must be. A loud thwanging bang into the door – where Lexi was. *Can't do anything... Must must must...*

Got to get back in... They're fifty yards maybe. Another loud thwang into the metal and I was back in the cab... gibbering I think. *Oh Lexi. Sorry sorry sorry...* Ramming it into reverse... *Try to drive it free going backwards...* It moved. Grinded. Gripped. Suddenly shrieked and roared. Tore. Awful noises, but it struggled backwards, and picked up speed. Sand loose under the wheels. Damnit – they were around us. So close. Rancid raving rabid faces. God it was pure doom. A hand coming in the side window. I tried forward. Tried to knock the hand away. Another the other side reaching to Lexi – She's shrieking. Then struggling against the hands pulling her hair.

Traction... *Forward. Thank fuck!* Shot forward. Knocked one over. Another trying to get in the vanished windscreen. Imagined I felt the bump as we went over him. Screaming – all of us, I think. *Must go forward...* Scrub too dense and tangling... Back. Hands clawing in

120

again… a gun exploded right in my face. Can't see or hear. I'm yelling at the hand – a face behind it, shrieking back at me. Mean. Ranting. Rotted teeth – desert tanned.

Grabbed at the gun… and wrenched and rammed the Toyota into drive. One blast. *Need reverse.* The gun barrel was in my hand – warm – that had never occurred to me. He'd fired it. 'Lexi! Lexi!!!! Here, Hold this. Pull the trigger. Point it at one of em. Any of'em. All of'em. Shoot the fuckers. I was ranting at everything from the maniacs all round to the gear shift lever. I pushed and pulled and screamed and panicked. I was useless and just doing things and crying and screaming and seeing another guy trying to get in through the ex-windscreen again. A maniac staring. A shout from him. Like I always thought a hyped-up druggy might be. God I'm fucking terrified.

Near on wetting myself. Sobbing with it. But I was keeping it moving. Backwards and forwards. Another almighty bang right in my ear. Another. Screaming again. They all got bloody guns? Yes – better forward. Sandy, then scrub undergrowth snapping and crackling. Shit!!!! Right in front – a wall of rock – the edge of a three-foot high rock bench.

Damnit! Back into sodding reverse yet again… Crashing backwards through the bushes. *There! The road. Where the tree was across. Got to steer that way.* It was going in reverse okay. *Maybe… just maybe…*

My head was silent. Except for the crashing of the scrub under the wheels… and the roaring engine… and me scream-sobbing.

No more gun explosions – that was the silence. And Lexi – she was quiet.

I looked down. *Shit No! She's dead. These bastards.* She was sagged down and dead. Couldn't see any injury

– but plenty of blood on her shirt and shorts; and her legs. Slumped forward, bouncing with the SUV's jolting about. Reverse is awful for any distance, but it was hardly going to matter where I went. *As long as it's not down a gully or anything... or get perched on a rock.*

Clear patch near the road and I spun it half sideways, damn-near rolled it, and was in forward in around a trillionth of a second... and sobbing more and going for the road past the tree block. And I couldn't breathe for the gasping and not believing when we got on the road and it was smooth and fast and getting us away. *Please don't have a vehicle. Easy catch me on a road they know...*

I'm looking all round. Ahead. Back. Sides. Down at Lexi. Blood all over us. *Soddin'ell.*

Nothing following... the road's empty in front. Empty behind us and I was crying and sobbing and seeing if Lexi was hurt or dead or okay and she was still down and sobbing just as much as me and clutching that gun like a hawk with a hamster.

We just kept going and didn't see anybody else... no other cars in either direction. I'm stroking her back and asking if she's alright. Hurting anywhere? 'Not shot are you?' *Oh fuck fuck no.* Not daring to pull up and get ourselves together.

How weird that was – I'd sort of calmed down by the time we got sort of safely clear. And Lexi was coming to, sitting up and stopping her sobbing, and looking round and she put the gun in the passenger door glove thing space and saying was I alright and, 'You look gruesome, Jeff.' And maybe she should drive and I said no I was okay and just a bit tired and she was insisting and pulling at me.

122

And I said, 'Okay just for a bit can't be far now.' She made me slide across and she went round and got back in.

And I felt sort of safe then. *Now Lexi's in charge. It'll be alright. God I been so scared for her and wanted to kiss her and hug her for being safe and still with me and it could have been so fucking awful for us.*

Yeah, that's how it was, how I felt. So completely relieved that Lexi was in charge now, so everything would be alright after I'd buggered it all up so bad.

I dunno a lot about the next bit. I was sort of awake but I was really tired. I'm good at counting my pulse. It's usually about 58 per minute, and I reckoned it was about that now... going lower and not as strong for a bit. Then back up to okay and a bit faster. So I'm alright, not going mad. Not dead. Getting slower, maybe.

'Is that it?' she was saying and poking me. 'See? Red roof in the distance? Couple of miles – two or three storey... old desert pioneer style.'

'Must be...' I was mumbling. 'Nothing else out here...' Too tired to look properly.

We pulled into the parking area. *A bit untidy with the parking*, I thought, but I didn't say anything... *best not upset her just now – she's sensitive about her driving.*

Then she'd gone and I was thinking I don't blame her. I'd have gone, too, in her place. Silly bastard gets her into trouble then panics.

I vaguely remember people coming all round me in the Toyota and wondering what they were looking at and mumbling about no windshield. Taking photos, too on their phones. Somebody was pulling at me and saying I was stuck to the seat and dragging at me. It sort of hurt and I was a bit unchuffed about that.

There was like a trolley they laid me on; and trundled me off and the reception area was cold, and dark-red-coloured with all these native hangings; and people mumbling and looking and taking pictures; and I didn't care and wished I had Lexi with me.

I'm all on my own. And I'm cold. And not seeing too good. Not inclined to move, so I'll stay here.

That seemed ages I was just lying and nobody near me and I was thinking things about ages ago like when I was a kind and some of the things we got up to, me and my brothers then Lexi *was* there and I was crying and saying I was sorry to get her into all that and was she alright now? And I wouldn't do it again and she was crying and saying don't be stupid...

There was this noise. Fast whumping. 'That's a helicopter,' I might have said. 'I've seen them on the telly.' But I didn't see this one...

Think I must have been on it. Remember it being next to me and being lifted up.

This police officer came to see me and he was really serious and I could tell I was in bother. He was saying about the people and I di'n't know what people and I was looking at the room and it was a sort of creamy yellow and had all wires and tubes and lights and I felt really stupid and lost in my head and wondering where Lexi was – *Left me, huh? Smart girl.*

'No, silly – I'm here.' Sneaking up behind me and wet-faced.

This police feller, he was saying about it all and it *was* serious, but I couldn't tell what he was on about but I knew Lexi would know.

And she did.

'Basically, Jeff. You killed three of them by driving over them – and I killed four with the gun.

'Durn. Y' beating me again, huh?'

'Mmm,' she nearly giggled a bit.

'Y' a good shot, eh? I'll have to watch it.' Struggled to speak. No breath. 'What they gonna do with us?'

'Medal, by the sound of it. The governor came visiting yesterday. He's running for re-election, I gather, and he was saying what heroes we are...'

'Time we got out of here, then, Mrs Penn.'

'Two things about that, Jeffrey Penn – *You* can't go anywhere 'til you can sit up, stand up and the rest – There's four bullet holes in you.

'And *I* can't go anywhere 'til they finalise the charges against me...'

'What? That gun? Shooting them. Tell'em it was me...'

'No. Not that. They're okay with all the shooting and stuff. It's just that I'm not registered as a driver on the rental agreement.'

'Oh. Tell'em all the damage was done while I was driving. And I got mad and made you drive.'

'Yes,' she looked a mite sheepish, 'I already did.'

HIGH-BABY

After an accident like that, seeing stars through the sunroof is hardly a surprise. What I'm not sure about is if they're up in the Big Wide Texas Sky, or in my Big Fat Stupid Head. 'Either way, I'm in the do-do's,' though nobody's listening right now.

'The only reason I'm looking through you at all,' I'm telling the stupid sunroof, 'is because my face is jammed up against you, so I ain't got anywhere else to look. All the trouble you've caused me today...'

I know the whirly bear will be landing soon, and they'll send out the care bears to come and get me out. Damn police know where I am alright – been following me for the past hour. Following from in front and down my side and ever'where. 'Dammit, I been stupid. I done wrecked High-Baby. And there ain't no getting myself outa here without no help...'

I only just fitted this new sunroof to my Dodge Pickup; it's the high-top cab model – the HiStyle. Like I told the guys, 'I need the raised-roof model cos I'm kind of a tall guy, and I got the extra padded seat, so I can really look down on the other folks.' Two grand it cost for the Panorama Vista version of my high roof, though I saved four hundred getting it fitted at Clack's Bodyworks.

It took four of us to lift it up there at the works. 'Hey Bub,' they're saying, 'this reinforced glass SunTop weighs a helluva lot; and it makes the cab eight feet from the rubber to the roof.'

'So let's use the engine hoist to get it in place, eh?'

127

'What I'm saying, Bub, is, she ain't gonna be as stable on the bends, so don't throw her round like you usually do, huh? That much weight, so high up. You need to be careful. You got to be real careful, making her as unstable as this.'

So, I listened without listening. Polite-like. But who's gonna attend to stupid things like that? Drive it easy? Who ya kidding? With Hi-Baby?

I went down Rodeo Jack's Saloon to celebrate the new high look, show it off. You know, where all the bikers hang out? We go there to rib up the two-wheelers in the bar, maybe run a few a bit close along the road. You know how you do, specially when you've had a few with the guys down in Abilene.

That new GlassTop was amazing – Huge view through SunnyBaby! All the way down there I could see the sky and the canyon sides, and… *Whee!!* Only just missed that eighteen-wheeler with quad stacks. I'm too busy watching the buzzards circling up there. 'But as long as you're still breathing, you're still truckin', huh?'

We had to roist a couple of black-leather bikers out the seats near the swing doors at Jack's. 'This's our side of the bar.' I tossed their baby ales out the swings and pointed'em the same way. Course, one of'em was all set to come at me, but I'm six-eight, and two-eighty pounds, so the low-forehead one was like placating him, and they shuffled over nearer the other bike-boys. 'You got the wrong dudes on for Abilene bikers,' I tell'em. 'Where's your chains 'n' badges, eh, Fruity Boys?' They looked kinda uncomfortable about that, watching the real bikers closing round them. Yeah, that was fun, stirring them all up.

128

So me and the boys had a few more Shiner Bocks and Lone Stars, and ribbed the server girls and the Bikie Boys… Giving'em what for on the wheely front, and we gives the challenge to the Bikies and they're chickening out – yelling and whooping – tossing a few drinks our way – all good-natured, like. Lot of laughing and catting – something about my new high rig. Jealous wannabees on Yamahas and Hondas.

A few more of the All-Black guys were in, 'New gang in town, huh?' I waved at'em, 'You wanna watch this pack of doo-lallies. There'll be blood before the night's out.' So I tossed some guy's ale at'em, and I was out of there.

'Yeah, let's swing this baby,' I sparked up, revved up and swerved out with a big smoky tail-spin, deciding I'd take my HiStyle up the ridge, and bomb it down Acantilado Canyon into Four Springs.

I made it there in twenty-five, no bother, and swung her round in the gravel parking lot at Gilo View; nice spray of gravel on a few parked chevvies. 'You can chase me if y' think y' can keep up,' I gave'em the bird and I was off down the Acantilado.

Four hairpins down and I'm swinging her like a tuna boat on rollers, and I see this whirly bear up there. 'I wouldn't have seen you without the SunnyTop, eh?' I'm pedalling the gas hard and he's coming in low and buzzing me. *You won't manage that on the tight stretches.* High-Baby was rolling them turns below Cayou Junction, where you get into the hard-rocking left-right, left-right rhythm.

I'm watching the flying bear through SunnyTop and she's really swinging it heavy. I can feel that extra-top-heaviness now, like they said down at Clack's, but I can't slow it down now… too winding to risk braking hard. Anyway, I ain't going to slow down; I'm too hyped, I guess. Plus watching this whirly bear with his cameras on me. Next thing, he's low in front of me and I'm looking at him and miss the turn a fraction and I'm skidding and she's spinning and we're cartwheeling over.

So frigging sudden.

So now here I am. I reckon most of them stars are in my head, and I just gotta wait for the bears to turn up and get me out… and Hi-baby's wrecked up. Aw, shit.

I hear'em coming… 'Yeah, you took your time,' I'm saying, except I got my mouth half full of SunnyTop, and I cain't talk so good.

One of'em's climbing up to see. He's grinning and dressed up in All-Black and my do-do's are just getting deeper and deeper. 'Hey, Bubba,' he's saying, like real quiet and low. 'Y' been a frigging pain long 'nuff, huh?'

And he's calling his low-brow to come up and see me, all grins, too. Dammit – I set myself up here, huh? And everybody else knew, except me, huh?

And they're having a low-whisper conversation and doing a share of nodding and big-grinning and I'm still kinda pinned and half-crushed under the glassite roof and the seat, and thinking, *Come on, y' pair o' jerks. Get me outa here.*

Low-brow's striking a match. 'Hey, smell that gas?' he says. Big grin.

'We better get clear, huh? Guess the guy didn't make it, huh?'

'Like that's a loss, huh? Pain in the butt, Bubba was.'

130

'*Was?* Hey, no. I'm still here. I'm okay. Come on guys. You gotta get me out of here, huh? Stop y' joshing, huh?'

From peering right in, close-up, one minute, they're backing off, and I'm still smelling the gasoline. They've climbed up on top, and I'm staring at'em through SunnyTop and they're grinning back as they light their cigarettes.

I just know he's gonna toss that match in here...

THE DRIVER WAS SHOT

"The driver was shot." That's all it said.
Headlines huge, page after page on Anita Q,
The pop-star queen who disappeared
When her car went off the road, her driver shot.
If Anita was kidnapped for gain,
Or wandered off, they didn't know.
Not a word about Ed;
Our child the driver, was gone.

The police burst in; the door smashed down.
Two thousand pounds that panel cost,
In Tiffany glass.
Didn't even knock or ring the bell.
A bellowing riot, and in they came.
We're sitting there, retired and frail,
Drowned in sorrow for our new-lost child.
We're a bungalow couple, in a village quiet,
Yet in they roared, faces raw and awesome wild.

Four with guns, they forced us back,
Shouting and shrieking.
Shocked near to death, we could only pray,
Our minds awhirl. Our home near wrecked,
Our comfy house, our peaceful lives
Bellowing, "Ed? Which room?" they stormed around.
And threatened more.
'Ed don't live here, and not for a year,' I said.
'Ed lives alone, just three doors down.'

They wouldn't have it. Not hearing a word,
They dragged us away in handcuffs both,
While all the avenue looked on,
With phones all poised to capture it.

133

'What do you know?' The demands snarled in.
'We're bound to discover each secret part
Of your offspring's life,' they said.
'And the crooked lies Ed's always told,'

'You're round the bend, the lot of you.
Our Ed's not like that…
Was not like that,' we cried.
They refused to believe.
They clouted me, again and again,
For some other truth to reveal to them.

They'd searched Anita's things,
Her emails, texts and notes.
Some plot within they claimed they'd found,
Revealing Ed had a life beyond,
Involved in a deal to kidnap and hold
This queen of pop – an aspiring movie star,
Anita Q, they'd found.

'You'll finish your lives in jail,' they said,
'If you don't tell us all you know
Of Ed's secret life and all the plotting
That's clear to see.'

'Let me see. Show me these things.'
I said, and wouldn't speak with them again.
They took their time, but eventually did.
I looked and saw and realised,
'You ludicrous pack of idiot berks,'
I wept and pointed out
Our Ed's a girl – Edwina Croft.

'All these plots are movie ideas that
Anita dear was trying out, like a kidnap plot.
Your Ed's a feller – See? Edward Fitzgerald-Lee.
Something went wrong on the road that night.

Our Edwina was murdered, driving along.
Your theory's half-baked, and daft as you.
Get out there and find
Your selfish queen of pop and screen.
She's the one who fixed this hype
For the sake of her own publicity.
You're blind to the real crooks here –
Anita Q, and Edward Fitzgerald-Lee.'

THE ARINGA DESERT WALK

Somebody came to me and he stood there looking round. He was in white. Everything here is white. He said something, but I don't think it was to me. He was standing high up, looming over me like a buzzard hovering. *So I must be lying down. I suppose that's why I can't move.* I did try to move. Several times.

People come, and I try to ask them where I am and what's happened. They say things but I don't hear. Or I don't understand, and they keep looking at something above my head… behind my head, on the wall. I think there are all sorts of electronic stuff there, with charts and equipment and screens and beepers. I thought I felt my arm move a bit when some women came and huddled over me. Then they went. I don't know if they said anything.

I was getting worried then. A big clock on the wall was going the wrong way. I saw people coming in through the window. Just floating in, and being in front of me, or over me. Some people keep looking at me and some not looking anywhere. *They say things, but it's just to each other.*

Maybe I slept. I dunno. Can't tell sometimes what's going on – every now and again, my bed lifts up and floats round this room. It's a ward. In a hospital. But that's a secret: they don't tell me.

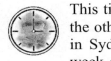I must have slept, because I had this dream. I know the place. I've done the Aringa Desert Walk lots of times. Hiking the Line, we call it. Can't get lost if you follow the rails out of Hanson Springs, over the dry river and straight into the Northern Desert.

It's a thing we do now and again, to prove we're still up to it. My wife don't mind; she's glad of the break, I suppose. Usually there's three or four of us.

This time, however, I was on my own because the other three were going to the All-Oz Finals in Sydney, and they'd be doing the walk the week after. 'But this was our original date,' I rowed with them, 'I booked my time off. I can't change it. Not without pissing off the boss and my missus – Sheila don't want me to get sacked from Lightworks. She'd blacken both my eyes this time.'

But they were adamant, 'We're going to the match, Jez. Got the tickets. Not our fault we won the semi.'

I'm three days out, walking the trail on my own. It don't stick right close alongside the rail line every inch of the way, cos y' not allowed to go over a couple of the trestle bridges, and there's a tunnel that seems to collect a bunch of dingoes. Anyway, who wants to be all shook up by twenty-thousand tons of train thundering past? I mean – there's one every day around eight-thirty a.m. And it cops the return around four in the p.m.

There're some nice little diversions off to weird Abo sites, and some cactus groves like don't grow anywhere else. There's a spring that feeds an oasis about as big a

138

dunny. And a grove of Ti Trees that smells like the waiting room in Langtrees – so I've been told, anyroad.

I suppose most folk don't like it on their own, out in the bush, but it never bothers me. Night out under the stars. No moon the first two nights. Pitch dark except for the stars. Not right silent, though. Must be a million creeperties putting on the style from sundown onwards. Suits me, it does. Done it often enough to love it, and not feel threatened. There're water points along the rail track every twenty miles, so you don't need to cart four gallons each like we did one time.

Three nights out. Fourth day, coming up to noon and I see something on the line, maybe half a k ahead. *Dead roo*, I say to my self – the stupid things never even see the trains, doing eighty. And the roo's doing thirty-five, and comes off second best every single time.

Maybe it'll be a dingo, I hope. Damn things – I carry the super-lamp with the flasher, a foghorn and pepper spray solely for them, just in case.

Except, as I get close. It's got blue and yellow on it. *It's wearing clothes. It's a person. I'm not gonna run in this heat*, but I walk fast, and I'm getting in a sweat as I get closer. Then seeing it like that didn't help: it was in bits. I took it real calm, even when it's obvious the head's missing. It looked awful like that. One arm was separated. Right leg was gone, too – three metres away. Blood was splattered all over the creamy-white cobbles. Outbacker clothes, same as mine when I'm hiking. It had to be suicide or murder. People don't get accidents when you can hear the train coming three miles away. Ain't all as deaf as roos.

No way was I going to touch it. I felt a bit vomity, but kinda fascinated as well. To see something like that. Miles from anywhere. On my tod. Surreal.

139

I slipped my tucker bag and tent-roll off and looked round. The head was there, four or five metres away, rolled down the slight embankment. It's not like it was anything to be scared of – it was a person. *Formerly* a person. Somebody I'd have chewed the fat with over a camp fire. I went to the head. Scraggy hair. Waterblue eyes. Stubble.

I was looking in the mirror. 'Shit. You're *me*. Spitting image.'

I keep trying to scratch my leg but my arm don't move when I feel down there. I'm not sure about any of this. I want to ask about the clock going backwards and where they were from when they came in through the window and why didn't they use the door.

There's one person who keeps coming. Claims she's my wife. She smiles and touches, stroking, like. Got a nice face, but I dunno. I don't trust her. There's these others who come; they reckon to be my sons. Don't remember that, though. Me? I don't feel like I got kids.

Another guy's been. Says he's my brother. A likely story. Drugged up as I might be, and befuddled in my thinking, I know I have no brother. No chance. So who is he? What's his game?

A couple of the white coats said he looks just like me, so I suppose he must be. So that makes three of us looking the same.

It was all fuzzy and hazy and cold. I was shaking and freezing. Another new person came and said things to somebody else. They clucked and fiddled with tubes and wires and screens; then I went hot-flushed, all warm washing through me. I think I moved my arm on my own. Think it was mine.

140

I reached down to the head – my head. I was intending to pick it up. Look after it. Maybe talk to it. It didn't seem right just lying there on its own. Middle of the desert, back o'Bourke.

I stopped: I shouldn't touch anything. I've seen enough cop shows on TV not to fiddle and contaminate the crime scene. Maybe there'd be fingerprints and stuff – DNA and that.

But the poor bastard was dead and he'd got no dignity like that. His head on the cobbles in the scrubby; and his body in mashed bits between the rails. It really wasn't right. What about his wife? or family? What were they going to think? Him left lying out in the sun, just baking up. Frying. I really felt shitty about that.

I wanted to move him off the tracks: the return train south was due in an hour or so. Not that it would do anything to this feller – he wouldn't be hit if a train did go over him again.

The trouble, I'm thinking, *is that there's no stopping the Redliner. Not with any kind of signal, or standing there waving. Drivers probably never look down the line from one hour to the next. All automatic these days, I expect.*

I checked my cell. Two bars, so it was half-full. Signal was weak and intermittent. I could try.

I managed to get a signal bounce after twenty minutes waving it round and walking about and trying triple zero… one one two… nine eleven… Got it! I told'em quick, which mile marker… the body. I said I felt bad about leaving him there. I should get him off the tracks. It just ain't right.

They were dead against it. Forbade me to touch him. *Me!* Not that I'm anybody, 'It's *me* who's here,' I yelled at my celly. 'I'm the bloke on the spot. I really ought to get him out of here. You want another train running over him?'

But they were having none of it. 'Can't stop the train – State Governor's aboard with his top team. Very tight schedule. Heading for Adelaide. We'll have somebody there asap', they said, 'before—' That was it. Lost the signal.

Yeah, right. Be with me asap? Like tomorrow, after Neighbours? They're not getting a helly out here, are they? Not going to kill this guy, is it? Being a day or so late collecting him. They'll allocate it to a medivan when it can be spared from tea-making duties. Probably watching the All-Oz.

That woke me up. *I really am on my own here.* I had a right sweat on. *That's me lying there.*

 Jipperty! I'm pouring with sweat. Seeing myself lying on the track. There's people around. I'm still on the tracks, iron rails either side of me. Faces looking down at me. Pulling at the rail – it's a grid… round my bed. They're getting at me; getting hold of me and pulling, wiping my head. I'm trying to stop them and they're holding me down and fixing things to me. But I gotta get out of here. Another train's coming soon. They're arguing with me and saying there's no train in here. Look… See? No trains.'

'It's a hundred k away,' I told'em. 'Coming fast. Be here at four. It's why the clock's going backwards again. I know. Need to move.'

But they weren't listening. 'Don't struggle.'

'You can't move yet.'

'We need to get these in you.' It's always what *they* need, isn't it? Pawing at me and sticking things in me –

142

like that'd do any good, with my head over there. Covering me up – big grey sheet coming over my face…

'Keep still,' they said in that voice like they're trying to soothe a nutter on crack, before they put him out for the duration.

Yeah, that's it… I'll cover him from the sun, but not move him. Not one inch.

I went back to him – the flies were out in force. 'Sorry, Blue. Coppers say I can't move you. Hard bastards back in Buggurum Bidgee, they are. Wish I could… Sorry.'

I spread my tent over him like a drape – I didn't think they'd like me erecting it on the tracks. Pegs wouldn't go into the cobbles, anyway. And the rail'd make a hard pillow, sure enough. My shirt over his head. I tried to see what he'd been thinking – like staring into his so-blue, so-dead eyes, 'What are you thinking now, eh, Brucie?

'What am I going to do now?' I really didn't like leaving him there – dingoes'd smell him before long. 'That'll screw their crime scene up.'

Well, if I'm staying here, I need shade.

I didn't have a spare tarp. And there wasn't a tree; no overhanging rocks; but, couple of hundred metres back I'd passed a culvert – a three-foot diameter concrete pipe under the track where there was an occasional watercourse. Yeah, there wasn't gonna be any flash-floods now, not even a hundred k upstream.

That would have to do as my shade until the cops got out here. I presumed it'd be cops; until they decided on cause of death. Cops and pathology folk. This guy needs attention; it ought to be today, if they're going to do any good. A night out here won't kill the me who's checking

143

for spiders, rats and scorps in the pipe. 'And it sure won't kill my other me, out there.'

There were quite a few creeperties in there. I was itching all over just to think of'em. So I wasn't sliding in there. 'Best I just hope the cops come soon, today. Or I'll have my tent back and pitch it next to him. He could have my shirt over him – where it ought to be, I suppose.'

'Stop scratching. Keep still. It's okay. It'll be alright.'

They're holding me down again. I can't have that. 'The train's coming soon. It'll run over me. I need to get away from the tracks.'

They're not listening. Just stupid voices placating me. All around me. Somebody talking too loud on his celly. Voices coming from everywhere. All telling me. None paying attention to me; what I'm saying. I need to move. Get away from here; off the tracks.

'I can feel it coming. It's the Redliner, heading into Hanson. I feel that tremble in the metal. I'll hear it soon. Very soon, the speed that loco travels at, it'll soon be right here. Governor and all. It'll be around ten seconds hurtling over me, past me, and gone with the wind.

Funny how you step back when a train's coming towards you. Subconscious, I expect, but there's also the wind blast off the front – a buffer wave, or whatever it's called.

I see Colin – Colin the Corpse – lying down there. It won't make any difference to him. Two hundred metres or so away from my culvert. I stood out there to watch.

Colin blew up. He exploded. It goes through your mind on the instant – my mind, anyway. 'What did he do

144

that for? The train must have gone over a trip down the track. Triggered a bomb under him.' Smoke puff. A crack in the air. Train was there. So fast-looming. It jigged up just a mite where the smoke was. The front dipped. It was off the rail. On my side. For about a millionth of a second, I was frozen. The Redliner was on me. I was in mid-air diving for the culvert.

I didn't quite make it. Some bit of it hit me. Rolled me. Wheel assembly, I think. It was roaring and slamming and hurtling all over me and round me. Deafening and thundering. I was right under it and terrified and sure I was gonna join Colin and get sliced, diced and mashed up. It was so damn loud and screeching and crashing. All round me, it was going on and on and on and it was all flashing sun. And shadows flickering and sparks flying. The whole ground shuddered and shifted under me and round me. The stink of rubber burning – where the Flamin' Jake did that come from? And metal burning. Something ripping and battering; rammed into the cobbles next to me – shoved me aside.

The worst of it stopped. The creaking began. Then some murmurs. Turning to screams and howls and a whole trainful of people dying.

 I'm lying here. Been an agonised age. Can't move any bit of me. What happened?

Coming to me... I'm under it - *It* being a carriage weighing sixty-odd tons. Must be full of smashed, traumatised and bleeding people. Yes... it's just that my legs are a bit trapped.

'We'll help you to sit up when you're a bit better. You're very weak. We need to keep you sedated – you're scratching yourself a lot. We've taped padded gloves to your hands.

145

'We need to get the infection under control...

'Hi, how y' going, Mate? Yeah – it's me, Todd... Your brother. Remember?'

I can't see him too well. Is it him they say looks just like me? Ugly bugger.

'You were on the rails.'

'Ha – they always tell me I'm off my rails, Mate, not on'em.'

'You remember what happened yet?' Was it him who said that? Or me asking him?

Remember. Do I? I dunno. 'Yeah,' I fuzzed my head a bit, 'I was lying on the track out at Goudgie Creek. And I found me there and I was all in bits. I watched it from the side, where my head was. I picked my head up and stared at me. Might have been you, though.' I studied him at length, 'They reckon we look the same.'

'Sheila's coming safto. She'll bring you a couple of sossie rolls with Vegemite; you got to promise not to get flakes and stains over the bedding – like you usually do. They won't let y' have a frostie, though.'

'I think it's the first time in my life I couldn't give a flying fart about a beer. I *must* be ill,' I told him.

He sort of nodded and said, 'Yeah, y'ave been a bit.'

'I reckon I do know you; you do look a bit familiar.'

Maybe he was still there when I slipped away again – Land of Nod, or Land of Comatose. If he was ever there in the first place, cuz I know he came floating in through the window and he thought I didn't notice. Real people don't do that. So I don't believe he's real, whether he's Todd the Brother, Colin the Corpse, or Another Me.

They've got me confused in here. Especially I'm confused about my arms and legs. I can see them – one arm, anyway. It's got wires and tubes in it, and it's strapped to a board that's clipped against the side rail.

146

Something keeps beeping; and there's ringing sometimes – that brings 'em running. That's up behind my head where they keep looking and poking.

To be honest, I can't actually see the rest of me, but there's a big mound over my legs with the blanket over it. I can wiggle my toes; and my calf doesn't half hurt sometimes. So I'm okay there. My left arm, though, I dunno where it is. I keep trying to move it and pick something up with it, but I get dizzy and can't remember what I was trying to do.

 I didn't know what I was doing. Not much of anything, actually: I must have caught a bang on my head, cuz I was like stunned. Also, I was stuck among all the heap of cobbles and metalwork. Buggerin' wheels were pinning me down so hard. I was *really* stuck: I needed to move the cobbles, get them out from under me. But it was a bastard to get hold of them: they were tight and hard and sharp and all round me and under me. Real struggle to reach them and get hold, and it was hurting so bloody much.

I was getting scared... and panicky. There was more stink of burning rubber. Or fabric, maybe; and diesel has this sweet smell. If that caught fire, I was deep in the fryer.

It was getting worse, the smoke. I was gasping and couldn't get enough breath to shout. The carriage I was under suddenly jerked and squealed. It slipped sideways. I squawked. It creaked again. Dropped down – so sudden! I nearly crapped myself. I was gonna get squashed or chopped up like me up there on the track by this chuffing great thing. It was less than a foot above me then, and stretching all directions, black and oily and dust-caked. I reached up and touched it. Didn't learn anything – not hot or vibrating. Except – I really *had* to get out from under it. Don't like being stuck.

I scrabbled and twisted and pulled and clawed at the cobbles round my legs, and it was knackering. One minute, and I was exhausted and no nearer to getting out. I had to sag back and just take a break – staring up at the black greasy massive machinery of this sodding great wagon right on top of me.

Time to re-appraise: twisting my head round, I reckoned I might be able to squeeze and wriggle to the left if I could move some lumps from under me. *Then maybe I can squirm down where the embankment opens a bit wider for the culvert pipe.*

So I need to keep wriggling and twisting, and reaching for a cobble and push it away. Then reaching round for another. And another.

My legs don't feel too good – a bit pressed-on – but I could move them. Managing to squeeze down and force, and drag myself out from under this huge great wheel mechanism – all shine and rust – massively-built thing with all the leaf springs and brakes and supports. It was dug into the cobbles right next to me, among all these heaped-up splintered sleepers and cobbles were heaped up all over the place, on me as well. *My ribs don't feel too good. Something sharp's not helping my breathing.*

But I'm okay. Survived it. Still trapped underneath, but I can wriggle, and scrabble down into a bit more space.

I think I passed out.

 I woke up. They were messing about with me. I thought it must be the emergency lot dragged me out from under that carriage. But I'm not on the trackside. I'm in a bed. It's two nurses.

Fussing over me. So, yeah, that's a sort of relief – means I got out okay. One of us did, anyway.

I tried to look what they were doing. Changing a bandage or something, I expect. Yeah, I didn't have anything on – a towel where it counted was all. And they were washing me. Flannels and wipes and dabbing with towels. Peering and touching. I could feel'em cleaning my feet... and my legs... fiddling about a lot.

I couldn't actually see my legs. I couldn't lift my head up enough.

And, I was thinking – all that train stuff was just a dream. Last time I Hiked the Line it was with Pete and Zobbo. Yeah, Alvin, too. Uneventful, as regards crises. Unless you count alcoholic poisoning and Zobbo getting clobbered by a bouncing 'roo that wasn't looking where it was going. Certainly no Redliner de-railing. Yeah, just a dream – must be brought on by whatever they've been giving me for... for... whatever I'm in here for. I was okay when I came in... er, when... well, sometime, anyway.

Thinking about it, I don't know when I came in here... or how, for that matter. Must have walked in for something... or was I in a road accident? Was I carried in?

I was waking up, and I felt so groggy and weak and aching everywhere and it seemed darker, except I could see red-orange flickering. Couldn't tell where, how far. And there was calling and shouting and crying and hysterics and calm and commanding – all the voices. I couldn't get a word out. And I was thinking – if I'd moved Colin, would the bomb have gone off?

149

I got to thinking it probably wouldn't. If it was set off by a switch when the train went over it two hundred metres up the line, then it wasn't going to blow if I cut it, or pulled the connection free. But would the emergency lot on the phone have listened?

Not likely – loved their rules, they did. A civvy pulling a lead out of anything? No way.

Ah, well, whatever; I got to move. Nightmare of clawing and dragging and it's getting harder and harder; and my legs are just dragging. But I'm getting nearer the culvert, and it looks like the fire's getting closer, and some screaming was getting louder... and shouting.

And I was scared of all the spiders and desert scorpions in there as well. Not that the scorps were bad, but the funnel-webs could be nasty little beggars.

But I just couldn't make it any further. Decided my legs must be broken cos they weren't doing much to help when I got inside the first bit of the pipe. Along with the sobbing I was doing, and teeth-gritting and looking at my fingers and they were all ripped and bloody... Hi ho – they'll heal. Get a few beers stimulating them.

Buggerit. I just can't get any further... I'm flat.

I'm flat in bed. I found out. They didn't tell me. When they went I got my arm off the bed bars that stop me rolling out. And I felt down. It was awkward with all that tubing, and I was in tight bandages and couldn't bend or twist. But I felt down there. There wasn't anything. My leg just finished in the middle of nowhere – like the rail line to the Gidge Bee factory that never got built.

This's definitely not a dream. I've lost a leg. Yeah, yeah, careless, I know. I was sure it was there when I came in. I remember walking in.

150

But now… I'm not so sure. I can't recall how I arrived here. It's definitely the hospital. Sheila confirmed that, though it was pretty obvious by then. They don't have all these nurses and doctors in other places that I know of.

The guy in the next bed, I thought he looked familiar. I asked him. He's Jefferson Allwhite – State Governor. 'I guess your schedule got messed-up, too?' I said to him.

'Huh?'

'You were on the train, weren't you? They said. It crashed… derailed… bomb went off?'

'Train? Bomb?' For a State Governor, he wasn't very bright. Echo Eric, more like.

'I picked up some food poisoning at a Filipino Burger Bar… No bomb or nothing. We were talking, me and you, yesterday.'

Yeah, like I'd talk with the State Governor – wrong side of the political divide, this one.

He was going on – they all do, these politicians, 'Thought I was rough,' he's telling me, 'but you – delirious and way gone. Hallucinating. You work in some place that uses mercury?'

'Lightworks. We use mercury in switches and lights and stuff.'

'They said there was an electrical fire – overheated some equipment – small explosion burst whatever you keep the mercury in – lot of concentrated vapour you breathed in. You collapsed down some steps; broke yer leg. Shouldn't do it, young feller.'

Sarky sod. I don't remember anything like that. He's wrong all ways up, this guy.

'You don't remember our chat yesterday? I told you about last time I came this way, down the Bidgee Rail Route on the way to an emergency meeting in Adelaide.

And you were telling me about when you hiked along that section to the north of here.'

'There was a train crash? It derailed.'

'Not that I heard.'

'No? Tell me then, smart guy, 'How many legs have I got down here?'

He was lifting up to have a squiz, 'Looks like the regular two to me.'

Huh. Politicians. Can't ever see what's in front of their eyes.

'You been dreaming, son. You sure been ranting. '

'Me? So have you. All the total rubbish you been coming out with.'

He was laughing, 'Yeah, how d'y reckon that?'

'Well, if you want chapter and verse, to start with, your social reform policies are total shite...'

I ARRESTED THE CAR

I was a tad nervous as I read the gleaming nameplate on his door – Eustace Lowdham, Notting County Sheriff. But… I needed to talk with him before proceeding with this incident. I could see through the wavy glass; he was busy polishing his silver badge and I didn't usually disturb him when he was doing that.

But I knocked, and walked in without any waiting. Best that way, I find, or he'll leave me out there for an age. Doesn't enjoy disturbances, Sherrif Lowdham; especially half an hour before home time on a Friday. He looked up from his decontamination labour – Jed Janevski vomited on him in Loga's Bar at noon. His eyes swelled by the bottle-glass wire-rims he wore. 'Better be good, Larry.'

That was a pretty dire threat, coming from him, and this time on a Friday p.m. I handed him the half-page ticket I'd written out – he can't interrupt that like he would if I read it out.

Two minutes it took.

He re-read it… turned it over. 'That it?'

'That's it, Sheriff; in a coffee cup. '

'I've got this straight, have I?' He summed up, 'A self-drive car crashed into another car, and was repeatedly battering into it against a wall?'

I nodded.

He continued, 'Shot at by a bystander… into the tires? And at the non-existent driver? He stepped closer and fired repeatedly into the electrics, reaching under the hood? He sees the wheels turning in his direction… empties gun into radiator… and it goes for him? Attempting to run him down?'

153

'You got it, Sheriff. I would obviously have arrested the driver under Sections 4—'

'I know the codes, Larry. Get on with it.'

'But there wasn't a driver. So I arrested the car itself.'

'In the name of John Doe?'

'Yessir, I kinda regarded the car as the personification of the unknown remote driver, who must consider himself under arrest and turn himself in. The penalties for evading justice mount on a daily basis. Arizona—'

'Larry.' He has that tone, late in the day. Fridays, especially. But I knew I was pushing my luck before I walked in.

'Several citizens who'd gathered around had that feeling, too, Sheriff. Kinda ridiculing me.'

'What about the passenger who rented the vehicle? Or is he the owner? Or an employee of the company. Can't you arrest him… her?'

'Lady. Unimpaired by alcohol or narcotic substances. Offered a demonstration ride by a would-be boyfriend who's an employee of the rental company.'

'So, who else could we charge? and what with?' Sheriff Eustace was on the verge of returning to badge-cleaning duty.

'The insurance company that certified it fit to be on the road? Or the state government that authorised experiments with driverless cars on public roads?'

'As I understand it, most states have codified the common law rule that a warrantless arrest may be made… they even included a misdemeanor vehicular violation.'

'My understanding, too, Sheriff, I believe the law originated among minor theft, prostitution, and playing card and dice games contraventions. Wouldn't really

154

want to be closely aligned with that level of history, would we, Sheriff?'

'Perhaps the designers, or builders, of the vehicle... the steering mechanism, sensors... brakes? The programmers in general? Or the one for that specific journey? Come on, there must be someone to hold responsible.'

Well, we could apply for an arrest warrant for an occasion in which the arrestee has committed a felony, although not in the presence of the arresting officer.'

'I was there, Sheriff.'

'Fine if we're arresting the car, but not for anyone else we hold responsible. We'd have to cite the Felony Persons Act – and roll them up with pickpockets, nightwalkers, gamblers and breachers of the peace.'

'All punishable, as a maximum, by a fine.' Minor felonies are my bread and peanut butter. 'If we deal with it under those rules, Sheriff, there's some vast corporation that would escape the deep examination that we can't provide.'

'Especially at the weekend,' said the Sheriff. 'That the right time? Five to six?' He turned the ticket over again, considering. Deciding, as the minute hand slid towards the hour. Home-for-the-weekend time.

'Aw, shit, Larry,' and he commenced tearing up the ticket. 'No crime.

'Pass it to the insurance companies to sort out.

'They get paid more than us.'

THEY FLEE FROM ME

'Me? Just hiking through. Hiking High Ridge.' The pair of locals were persistent, kept commenting on my City-Boy look, and asking, 'How come you're here?'

'Where y' from?'

'Y' come to a little roadhouse diner and tavern middle of nowhere like this?' They drained their early-morning beers in synchrony and stared down at me.

'Why y'interested? Something to hide? I ain't no revenuer... can't even spell TTB. Just hiking High Ridge.'

'With no gear? Saw you come in last night – no back-pack when you checked in the motel room. Paid cash, too.'

'And y' name's Thomas.'

'*Wyatt* Thomas.' He sniggered like my name means something funny.

'Think y' Wyatt Earp, do y'?'

'Yeah, looks like a sharpshooter, don' he?'

I sighed. It wasn't the Cochise lawman I was named for; it was some English Lord called Sir Thomas Wyatt. I guess my parents knew something about him. But these guys? Best play along with them; don't want no trouble, 'So what is it? Y' brother owns the motel and y' looked at the register? So you know my name.'

I finished off the eggs, checked the coffee pot. 'I stashed my pack up on the ridge. No point humping it all down here and back up again this morning. I saw this place from Hendrix Point; came down for a hot meal; and a bed appealed, too. Mighty comfy it was. That okay with you guys?'

'Where y' heading?'

'Along the High Ridge Trail, like I said. That way. East, to Chilhaw.' *Never tell the truth.* I sighed again; I do sighs kinda heavy and exaggerated. *Come on guys, off my back, eh? I'm not one who likes to be seen and spoken to, or of.*

I concentrated on my plate, avoiding eye contact. Looking them in the eye just encourages confrontation. 'I'd just like to finish my beans and burger in peace, guys. And grab a coffee to go. That okay with you two, huh?'

'Y'ain't even got a change of clothes. There's a mini-shop in the filling station.'

'I saw. Got me a toothbrush is enough,' *Why do I talk like that when I met Appalachian folk?*

Grinning and muttering, they swaggered away, fresh beers in hand, down the bar end of the dusty diner.

I kept a wary eye on them: two check-shirted guys, both bigger than I am. Baggy jeans and a stink of old aftershave. The juke box suddenly blared out with a mindless rock city blast that made me wince. *How'd they know I hate that kinda stuff?*

I tolerated it until I'd finished the hash-browns, and the coffee pot was drained, then relocated to a far corner seat with a bottle in a bag.

'Y'ain't allowed to drink y'own,' I was informed by the fairer-haired one of the swaggering duo.

'It's Energy Four. He bought it out the mini-shop, Jake. It's okay.' The barkeep tried to help.

'Mind y'own, Charlie,' he was warned, and Redneck One re-approached me.

'You was here before; recognise you, don't we Hose?'

'Sure do,' Redneck Two swung off his bar stool and brought his beer over. 'You ain't no stranger here. We reckon it was you who caused all the bother 'bout a

158

month ago. When Maise-Lou got attacked. Beat up good, she was. That you, was it? *Wyatt Thomas?'*

'Beat on her, did you, Boy?'

'I've never been here before, I told you—'

'You don't tell us nothing, *Boy.* Nobody tells us nothing.'

I managed to suppress the upcoming sigh. 'I'll be going now, Gentlemen. You'all have a good day now, huh?'

That wasn't good enough for Jake and Hose: one blocked my way, the other put a hand on my shoulder to keep me seated. 'Well, guys—' I started to rise. A fist in one's belly and a rising headbutt under the other's chin laid them out on the scuff-tiled floor. I was up, paid for the breakfast with a sawbuck, 'I'll be away now, Charlie. Keep the change.'

Halfway across the empty parking lot, I heard their voices behind me, the diner door crashing back, their half-drunk, enraged shouts disturbing the distant birds' chorus; and me. I turned, and watched them stumble towards me. Changed their minds, stopped and headed for an SUV, grabbing into the back for— *Yes, I knew it – rifles. Long-barrel two-twos by the looks – old squirrel guns.*

No point taking chances with bravado – I ran for the wood.

Two shots fired – one immediately, and vanishing without trace. The other, at forty yards, hit my left shoulder, pushed me off balance, and sent me rolling into the wet-slicked skim of mud. *Damn. He's either lucky, or a sharpshooter with squirrels.*

I was back on my feet, *The blood's a nuisance, but the pain's minimal for now. Arm movement isn't restricted*

159

yet, but could be. It'll need attention later. Meantime, I'm outa here.

On my feet and into the wood. Two more shots. One slapped into the back of my left leg, spun my balance and I was down again. Heard their howls of delight, but was up straight away. A glance back. They were coming after me. Persistent pair of pine-boys. *The leg's not too bad. Can feel the pellets... they'll come out... Damn again – it'll bleed.*

The trees were sparse for the first few moments, then the undergrowth thickened up and it was a matter of finding routes through and up – deer and hiker tracks. Out of breath, more through pellet shock than the running, I took a moment to rest and size up the situation.

On the edge of the lot below, the two check-shirts were staring up, searching. One spotted me, pointed – shouted.

Damn, hawk-eyed assheads. *Yeah, they seen me alright. So what they gonna do now?* I watched'em. They dithered, did a bit of yelling, and were joined by four others – two young guys; two a bit older, maybe. Pointing up to where I was still resting up, tying a kerchief round my thigh. Not much blood yet. No big prob.

Something decided, two disappeared across the parking lot. *They gonna be coming up here soon. I need to move... Arm and leg stiffening up already.*

So, a mile-long climb up to High Ridge...

The going was hard, strewn with loose twigs, tangled with creepers and blocked by dense patches of under-scrub. Ten minutes of hard climbing, I needed to rest again – leg bleeding too much. The tie needed re-knotting, some packing.

And that was when I first heard the howling yap of the hounds. Concentrating, I reckoned three, maybe four.

160

Okay... depends what they do with'em – turn them loose and try to corner me? Tree me? Not going to happen.

Back to the climbing and scrambling. Hearing the voices, shouting to each other... calling to the hounds. Closer... closer... Okay, stay calm. Hunting knife out my back-belt, and wait against moss-buried rock face – *they can't surround me here.*

One at a time, the hounds arrived. I never heard of them being bright and organised. Good. The fore-runner leapt, straight onto the blade, piercing its broad chest and flattening me against the rock. I got a second hard stab into its ear, and it was down. The second was right behind; just as unthinking, leaping for my arm. I whipped round on him, swung the blade, and opened a huge gash down the side of its right jowl. It stumbled, came back, lost its throat and collapsed, bleeding profusely, chest heaving.

The other one – no, two – were more circumspect – acted together. One suddenly lunging for my arm, the other going for a leg – but they weren't trained in fetching people down – more like retrieving squirrels, or keeping hold of a deer until the masters arrived. The one locked on my knee went down to three hard blades straight into the back of its neck... again... again. And the last one – *I hope* – dropped free of my arm as the blade lashed into its eyes.

That had me breathing kinda heavy. Okay... listen out... the voices were only fifty... forty yards away. Sounded encouraged by the hounds' baying. They'd be bothered now by the silence. No time to rest longer... Maybe ten seconds before they're here, and in the sights of their guns. *At least they won't have their dogs to track me; although they're probably as good as the hounds on this terrain.*

161

Scrabbling and scrambling, both legs now slowed and stiffening; left shoulder and hand both bleeding. Be useless soon... damn them. Need my backpack... Fix things.

The laughing, confident voices reached the mossy rock, and changed to yells of rage... of revenge and hatred. Holy Loley, they're pissed alright. Maybe won't think straight – not that they been doing much of that so far.

Two... three shots come echoing through the trees... A few leaves spinning down. Un-aimed anger-shots; statements of intent. 'We'll have y' schlongs off, Boy. Long and slow is how you go...' It sounded like their regular mantra.

A swift glance down the slope, and all around. Endless trees. No sign of how much further the High Ridge trail was – *Could still be half a mile. Five hundred feet vertical, likely. Must get the backpack; be gone from here, before they have a clear shot. That smeghead in red check's a dead-eye with that Long Tennessee rifle.*

Usually manage this kinda climb with no bother, but I was rasping and gasping, damn squirrel guns. I headed up the slope, with the advantages of being fifty yards in front of my redneck pursuers; and them not having the hounds any longer.

Yeah, but I got my own disadvantages, with the two rounds of squirrel shot, and blooded twice by the hounds' teeth. Plus not knowing the terrain as well as they do.

Strength near spent, I was stumbling onto the high trail along the ridge, rising slightly to the left. *Yes, that way. I passed this fallen juniper. Back pack's not too far.*

Stumbling, gasping, chest agonised with the forced breathing. Everywhere ached. I'd dropped my knife

162

somewhere – fallen from frozen fingers. *Damn this. I'm no Rambo. Need my pack. Get out of here…*

Damn assbrains spread out, gonna cut me off at multiple points. I could drop down the other side. Precipitous, though. And there ain't nowhere to go – no settlements down that direction.

There! There, ahead, yes – two fallen spruces, crossed each other. My pack's under the cross.

It felt like my last, ultimate ounce of strength that saw me staggering up the last thirty yards of the trail to the spruces, saw one of the searchers step out a hundred yards ahead, looking both ways. He shouted, waved. Damn, keep going towards him, ducking off the trail into the scrub and working my way to the shelter of the spruces.

Quiet… I'm not visible here. Quiet… Bag uncovered… unzip. Oilskin case out. Click it open. The relief. *Too early for relief,* I'm telling myself, *still ain't out the woods.*

Ten seconds to clip the barrel onto the stock. *Usually do it in four… shaking too much.* Another ten to twist the silencer in place – *no point alerting all of them at once.* Only one clip of bullets – ten. *Have to make them count.* They slammed comfortingly in the breech and it was so satisfying to cradle the weapon and cock it into single-shot.

Now. Rest. Wait. Let the first ones seek me out. Ha – I bet my English namesake never had this much trouble – being a poet and ladies-man. Although, being in the court of that Henry Eight can't have been all fun, not with Henry's head-chopping habits.

I could hear at least two closing in along the trail… calling to each other and to me – Fools. Still with confident bravado and dire threats what they were going to do with me. 'City Boy,' one was exulting in his skill and country sense over me, 'We gonna whup you out y' skin.' *Sounds like Green-check Shirt, the darker-haired one from the diner.*

One's very close, poking into the brush next to the bigger of the spruces. Yes… there he is. Twisting to kneel up, I took careful aim and blew someone's chest apart from five feet away. His thud on the ground was louder than the discharge. They call it a silencer, but it's more of a muffler – just deadens the report and cuts the flash out.

Two of his companions are heading close now – one from each side. Wait… wait… Easy… Rifle poised, I stood, adjusted slightly, and dropped one through the chest at twenty feet. Turned and took the other the same, twenty feet on the down-trail side. Satisfyingly surprised look as he realised, and went flying back.

Okay, so it's started… Patience now, Wyatt. I waited. The others'll be along soon, still too stupid to creep and sneak.

Except – one was right here, weapon raised, older guy, snarling something at me. That verbiage took him two seconds and cost him his life as I fired from the hip at the same time, and we both flew backwards. Him with a hole through his sternum, and me with the recoil while I was off-balance.

Corner of my eye, a flash in the background – fifty yards down the trail. That was Dead-eye firing… Red-check by his side?

Eased back to my feet, swaying, alert for the murderous pair of Hillbillies, I stood, real cautious. Peering down… nothing. I stepped out, making a target of myself. Nothing. No movement. *They're either creeping up, or running down. Back where they came from. Can't be having that.*

164

Keeping the gun at the ready, I looked down the slope... heard the shouts and crashes. Yes, both of them, scrambling down through the trees. *Damn. I best take care of them, I suppose, or they'll have the law up here.*

I steadied myself against a Virginia pine, took careful aim. One perhaps a hundred feet down, and thirty to the side... dodging and scrambling between the trees. Had to have a little smile, 'As my English guy wrote, "They flee from me that sometime did me seek."' I fired. The bullet splintered bark off a tree that leapt into my line of sight as I followed the figure tightly downwards. Another. The same. *Take a deep breath. Course, my English feller said it about the women round Henry's court, when he was getting on in age; not a couple of rednecks chasing down a hillside.*

Four cartridges left... Open space coming up. They've wisely kept apart until now, but they're both coming into the same exposed area – sparse grass, no trees.

So my next shot took the furthest runner through the middle of his back, and he went sprawling down the rocks. A second later, the last one went down the same. *Okay, just wait and see...* Studying the bodies down among the trees, the last one twitched. Just once. Single shot blew his head into fragments.

Okay, so now I gotta fix myself; need to be in Morganville this time tomorrow. See if one of these guys has a decent blade... get these pellets out, cleaned up and tight-wrapped.

Cleaned up and fit, I took one last gaze at the unmoving bodies, 'I guess that Thomas Wyatt guy knew his stuff, hanging round with that Henry Eight. He bumped off near as many wives as I done.'

Hump my backpack on, ease my shoulder padding, 'Now I only got one bullet for tomorrow's job. I better hope the State Governor don't run as fast as them two.'

IGOR

As I told the bloke trying to squeeze in, three cars down, 'Igor, our traffic warden is very keen, paid by results, six-feet-five and a body-builder. So you don't cross him, not by an inch or a minute, or you're dead – and broke. Only stay one hour, not a second more. And it's four quid in the metre, over there.' I pointed.

I was already parked on the end of the short-stay section on the High Street, my front bumper dead level with the start of the double yellow bars. I climbed out and admired the accuracy of my parking before watching this bloke defy the laws of space and motion by parking in a gap that tiny.

'I'm sure Igor memorises every single vehicle's expiry time and strides between them to be on hand exactly on time. He's a record-holder for bookings in a day, in a week, a month... and for power-lifting down the gym, where he's twice been voted "Most aggressive member" by a highly cowed, tongue-in-cheek membership.'

I left Tight Parker to his squeezings-in, had him classified as a future victim for Igor, and checked my shopping list – to be completed within fifty-seven minutes.

So, I finished my shopping. *Great, I'm a minute early,* when I arrived back at my car.

Ah. A minibus-sized van had parked right in front of me – on the double yellows. It was one of these with a single, big back door. He'd left it gaping wide open.

Must be delivering something big close by, I assumed, *and hadn't bothered to close it if he had his hands full.*

But, I looked, the wide-open rear door was only six inches from my front end. There was no way I could get out. *Igor's coming – thirty yards down the road. Panic... panic... He'll do me.* I slammed the van door shut and leapt safely into my car, really pleased I had enough space to get out now.

'That'll do nicely,' I said to myself. 'I'll be able to swing out at that, and Igor can book him – nice juicy fat Double-Yellow Fine for his bonus packet and—'

And that was when the high street erupted. Three men came hurtling past me – nearly had my wing mirror off. They grabbed at the back door of the van, jerked. Pulled. Twisted. Cursed. Dropped their bags down to twist the handle undone with both hands. *Oh, dear, having a problem with it. Shouldn't I have shut it?*

Not that I cared – I needed to get away before my last half-minute was up.

I admit I was shaking and panicking at the thought of Igor. *He'll be persecuting me – again.* So I started up – quick as I could. They were still yanking at the rear door. *Must need the remote to key it open,* I was thinking. *They're totally stuck. Igor's upon them.*

One of them leapt towards the driver's seat. Igor got to him. 'You don't get away from me like that,' he shouted, and slammed the door on the would-be driver's leg as he tried to get in. In full pontification mode, Igor had his notebook out; camera swinging; attitude on public display.

The other two went for him. I slammed into gear, thinking I've got to be well gone before he books me, as well. A mite distracted, though, I just shot straight forward instead of swinging out into the road. Smashed into the back of their van. *Shit shit shit.*

**

168

And so it was that Igor and I hit the front page of the local rag. 'Hero pair defeat bank robbers!" the headline ran. I was credited with quick-wittedly closing off their retreat by driving close enough so they couldn't open the rear door, and pinning three bags of cash to the road under my wheels. Igor got the plaudits for "quelling three violent thieves without thought for personal safety."

'Without thought?' he told me when our interview was finished. 'I wasn't missing out on a bonus catch like that: I got them for parking on Double Yellows; and *you* for the same, plus overstaying a One-Hour Limit.'

'But... but... Igor, darling,' I protested, 'I wasn't over time, or parked on the double yellows.'

'Dorothy, dear lady,' he said, when we eventually arrived safely back home, 'when you moved forward and hit the back of their van, your front end was on the double yellows, and the rear end over-stayed its time in the parking space.

'Anyway, what do you have planned for tea, my dear?'

FRAGMENTS OF BOXING DAY

It was Christmas Eve and I was mellowly drunk but walking fine. Heading home down Thirty-second for a bleak on-my-own nightcap bottle of gin. My dad might or might not be up. He hadn't wanted to come down Finnegan's Bar with me because he was sure I was meeting my supposed boyfriend – he still didn't believe I ditched Jake the Bastard weeks ago.

Okay, so it's risky walking the dark streets that time of night on my own, but – a. it's Christmas, b. I did self-defence, c. what's the chances? d. round here? Fifty-fifty. That's my joke for the day. Well, it'll have to do. Like I was saying – I had a drink and it's Christmas. And anyway, have you been down Thirty-second late night? You'll know then.

That was when I saw this figure coming at me. I assumed it was a man, but he was all stumbling and nearly falling off the sidewalk and kept reaching out in my direction. Funny, innit? I've seen that happen on TV and the woman always shrieks, screams and has histrionics – in that order. Except me. I was full of Christmas cheer. Well, Christmas drear, more like. And I thought, What the Fraggle Rock, and took a few steps towards him, sort of thinking I'll sort this scroobie out if he tries something. I was full of Christmas spirit like that; and Christmas beer, too – Finest Port City IPA.

'I'll have your balls for earrings if you so much as—' I warned him, as I was getting close, but he was nearly on his knees by then. All wild-eyed and gasping – and that was just me. Okay, yeah, him too. He was falling onto me and I backed off, quick-like, 'Watch it,' I warned him, 'This's Thirty-Second; we got the gutter for the likes of you.' Sure seen plenty of'em. Right, yeah, me included coupla times.

But this wa'n't no trick to grab me or nothing. I was still really wary like, but he was genuinely out of it. The eyes were gone, all glazing in and out, Well, both his eyes, not all of them, exactly.

He was garbling something about been drugged and kidnapped, and he'd escaped and, 'They are after me.'

I was thinking what a load of whatnot, and I said, 'Who in the dungheap would want to kidnap a specimen like you?'

So he says, like, 'My father's Lord Somebody or Other at the embassy, and—' He fell down about then. I recall landing not far away when I was out with Jake one time. Or was that Thirty-fourth?

'Somebody wants me,' he was burbling away.

'T'ain't me,' I said, and I was thinking what a snooty posh accent he got, and I sez, 'Y' sound like y' queen. Jolly Assholing Dee.' Okay, but the guy was in trouble – really, he was. And it was Christmas and all that crap.

Well I don't know what to do, do I? I mean, I never— Well, not that often. 'Anyway,' I told him, 'just remember it sure ain't me who wants you.' So I dragged him up on his feet and starts walking him down Southridge Avenue. Though, really, I had to make him hold on and, basically, I just dragged him back towards home. Much like I did with Jake the Legless a few times.

Oh, yeah... *that* was the place... me and Jake were in the gutter just there. I told him, but he wa'n't listening. In fact, this guy's getting worse and jabbling things and falling more. And I kept having to hoist him up and we nearly fell over and I had to topple him up against a tree and read him the Ninth – about everybody's got the

172

right not to be mauled about by some drunk, so just watch it, Buster. And just wait to get my breath back. Brooklyn! He was hard work, especially the state I was in.

So we're there, up against this tree on the corner where Thirty-second crosses Bailey, and I'm keeping tight hold of him, and his eyes are alternately glazed and shut. And his head keeps dropping on my shoulder and some guys are coming past and I don't really like to look round – I got a sort of feeling. But they hardly looked at us against this tree, thinking like we're making out, I expect. So I spare'em a swift glance, casual-like. They got guns! Out. And waving'em! They're like The Godfather meets Goodfellas. Come on – this is Washington, not Windy City.

So I kept him there. The snogging was like with a dead seal – the fishy sort, not the army ones. SEALs are worse.

But these guys keep coming back and looking pretty riled up and waving guns and peering at us and I told'em, 'You get in line, boys. You can have your turn next.' So they said something foreign, and pistoled off back where they came from.

O'sefat! But he was hard work to get that last hundred yards. Dad had gone to bed, so me and this heap of a drugged-up feller sort of fell in there and by the time I got my coat off and fed the cats, he's powed out solid on the sofa. So I ended up drinking gin with a guy who never even realized he was in such brilliant scintillating company.

I stuck some stupid over-the-top so-called comedy on the TV – Comedy Central channel, course. And laughed myself silly and didn't really need six different gins.

They made the next film even unfunnier, but I was dying laughing anyway.

So dad found me sometime around midday snuggled up with this guy – like whose name I never even knew then. But it was okay. Dad was getting the huge dinner ready and there was tons of it, like always. And we got this guy sitting up, and practically showered him with his clothes on and dad dressed him in some of his stuff. So we stood him up. Then sat him down at the table with some red wine. Okay so that wasn't the best idea in the world, but nor's Christmas. It's Friday nights that're God's best idea.

New guy drank a sip. Looked glassier-eyed. Ate some turkey. Passed out again. Me and dad did too, and had a bite of turkey and dill when we woke up. And dad said, 'It's time for gin. Yes, it is. Because I didn't get any last night.'

That was when I wondered, 'Did I get any last night?' I looked at Pass-out Boy and wasn't too sure. Probably not, state he was in.

Dad was glad I'd found another boyfriend – even a semi-permanently comatose one.

It was really late when we dumped the guy in bed – my bed – and I stayed down there on the sofa.

Then, next morning, it's Boxing Day and we just pig out and it's my turn to cook the dinner and do the sandwiches and stuff for tea and we stick some DVDs on and sleep. And it all drifts by in gin for me and beer for dad.

This guy is called Hubert. *Hubert!!!* I ask you – Hubert!! What a dork of a name. But he's okay and he's coming round and scared about it all and keeps thinking maybe we kidnapped him and we showed him the wide-open frigging door and said, 'You can screw off whenever you like, Hubert. Turn left out the door, and close it behind you.'

But he's like a rabbit and he fidgets and stays and hardly knew what was going on all Boxing day. He'd been on something, alright, and was taking his time coming out of it. 'Like Fragment Man, in't he?' Dad says. 'He's just getting fragments of a day. Probably still thinks it's last Thursday.' It din't matter, of course, cos me and dad were fine on the gin, leftovers and TV.

Then next morning – maybe the morning after – we see the news on TV. And he's on it. 'It's your Hubert,' Dad pokes me.

'Still no leads,' Lester Cronkite is saying, trying to look puzzled and caring. Yeah – like he ever succeeds in either. 'Thought to be kidnapped... probably dead.' Father with stiff upper English lip. It did wobble a bit, but really, he was good at it – gutsy old guy.

So anyway, course, we had to phone somebody and they all came roaring up with sirens going like Old Salem. It took a bit of explaining, and me and dad got taken in under the Patriot Act. The Patriot Act for Shit's Sake! Wait till I tell'em down Finnegan's – talk about street cred. I don't know anybody who got themselves arrested under the Patriot Act. I won't have to buy a drink in there all winter.

So right. Hubert eventually said we were okay and he was piecing together what happened. 'Though I can only recall fragments of Boxing Day. Or was it... er... whatever the other day is. How long have I been gone? and nothing before... At one time I was in LA with a gang of prostitutes...'

Yeah, right – that was the movie we had on, and he passed-out around half-way through, just when we were getting friendlier…

Plus – me and him, like, we're still kinda close; and getting closer; especially as Little Lord Half-English Fauntleroy is due late September.

Well, you know how it is when you've had a few…

And it's Christmas…

And you've been watching a movie like that…

LIONESS

Our first trip abroad with the children, apart from camping in France. But this was...

'Flying? *Wow!*'

'...to Egypt? *Wow!*'

'...for a cruise? *Wow!*'

So the girls were happy, and we booked for early in the year so it wasn't excessively hot for three little blonde waifs, and Jill, a slightly taller blonde waif. They'd suffer if it was too hot, but Louise, my eleven-year-old, was desperate to go, because of a project she'd been doing in school.

'Dad! Dad! I know all about it! I'll be able to tell you all about everything.'

'That's something to look forward to,' I congratulated her, 'although I expect we'll have a really nice and knowledgeable guide to help us as well.'

The staff aboard the Royal Anubis were a great bunch – nearly all men, happy grinning faces and quick jokes. They'd bring out a cake amid trumpets and songs at the least excuse, or with no excuse most evenings. They also helped to prepare the kitchen food and they cleaned the rooms. On occasion, they'd apple-pie someone's bed, or, 'Dad! They've laid flowers and biscuits on my pillow!' And they were ready with cold towels and a drink when we returned after a dusty day seeing the awesome sights of the ancient world.

Even Joanne and tiny Melissa were loving it – including all the attention they attracted from the crew.

They teased the men back, and they were all making a great game of it to entertain themselves and each other.

'I am your escort and guide. I will be with you each day. I am Menhit.' She was a young woman with striking looks – so classical in face and complexion and traditional dress. Black long hair with a sheen like no other. She was a beauty, alright. And she knew it, and used it. She was much respected by the staff, and probably feared a little, too. They all seemed to be very careful of her; almost subservient. Especially when she pointed at them. She did *pointing* so meaningfully.

'You can see them quake,' I whispered to Louise.

She tried to dominate the tourists in her care in a similar way. 'I shall give you your instructions each evening for the following day.'

It was reiterated as strict orders in the morning, with thorough checks that we had our sunhats, water, and sun cream with us. 'You need to be looked-after. You are not accustomed to the sun and heat. You will burn.'

'I think that's a threat more than a prediction,' I whispered to Jill. 'She missed the "in hell" off the end.'

'Only if we don't obey her. So you behave yourself.'

'Menhit was the name of a Nubian Goddess,' one of the staff whispered, when he saw us looking at her dubiously. '…the Goddess of War, the Lioness.'

Louise Googled the name, Menhit. "She who massacres", she read.

'That's a bit worrying, isn't it, Dad?' Joanne gazed darkly round – but she's a bit of a drama queen.

Menhit did *not* approve of photographs, insisting that everyone must fully attend to her rhapsodising about *Egyptian Genius and Wisdom* at every ancient site from Aswan to Zau. Well, between Aswan and Luxor, anyway. Judging by her haughty lip-curling around our group, there wasn't one of us who measured up to the genius of *The Ancients*.

'Nowhere near,' I muttered to Joe and Serena on the breakfast table.

'She's simply proud,' Jill defended her.

'Arrogant,' I said. 'She sees herself right up there in the midst of all that genius. If not above it.'

'Well, she does share a name with a goddess.'

'Huh. Menhit, the Goddess of War. Right.'

'It's *everso* interesting,' Louise looked up from her notes.

'Propaganda,' I said, 'Indoctrination.'

'She's lovely and I wish I had hair so long and black and shiny,' Joanne sighed.

'It's dyed,' I grasped at straws.

'She held my hand walking up that slope,' Melissa told me, in aloof defiance.

'Trying to imbue her influence into you by direct contact.'

'Silly.' Melissa had the final word. She often does, especially at night.

Defeated, I looked at them, lined up against me in size order against the stern railing, like four blonde steps. 'Okay, stay still a mo, and I'll take a pic with the river and the palm trees in the background.'

179

Menhit's everlasting evangelising at Esna, and Luxor, constantly extolling the magnificence of Egyptian scientific and cultural history, was becoming a wee bit too much. 'The greatest, most creative and inventive Empire the world has ever known.' It was wonderful how she could brag and sneer at the same time. But I had a new camera, and wanted photographs of these great sites and sights, not deep inner knowledge and appreciation. So I sneaked out the back of each temple with my camera, waving in queenly manner towards the ladies, 'It's in the hands of my secretarial team,' I grandiloquised when Menhit noticed and paused accusingly.

The Goddess of War *really* didn't like that: she launched into an undeclared war against me, beginning with that night's party – there was some kind of party every night aboard the ship, someone's anniversary or birthday; or Easter; a gala to welcome new guests. Games, singing and alcohol; comedy sketches by the crew; dancing and processions; cakes, karaoke and guest spots by anyone who felt like singing or telling jokes.

It was our tenth anniversary, me and Jill – tin. All the staff came parading in with paper trumpets and a gift, thoughtfully provided by Menhit. I smiled at her, but her face looked as though she accepted my super-pleasant smile and nod as a threat. The gift was so light and delicate as we unwrapped it – an empty can of Diet Coke.

'It's tin,' she smiled. 'Perfect for *you*. And I have something special for you. No, only you, not lady.' She waved Jill to remain seated, and crooked *that* finger for me to follow.

Well, you just know when you're in for it, don't you? But, what the hell – I'm on holiday. I went where she indicated, and managed to turn the staff's artistic dance into a comic routine with my way-over-the-top incompetence. Menhit didn't like the laughter being *with* me, instead of against me. She glared and muttered threats as she led the applause at the end. The photos on the board next morning were great – Jill bought one of each.

Of course, I lost the draw for something the following night, and had to do the forfeit – hopping in a circle whilst drinking and singing. 'That's nothing,' I told her, 'I was a student in Hull. We all did that for four years.'

The same with being blindfolded and persuaded to stick a tail on a donkey with a pin. You can tell from the giggling that it's not a donkey any longer. The balloon's bang was a bit of a surprise, so I fell over backwards and did a reverse roll.

'Don't overdo it, Dad,' Louise muttered. 'You *must* have known it was a picture of a naked lady you had your hands all over.'

'How? It wasn't a 3D picture.'

So that was the way of it for the first few days and nights along the Nile. Beyond Aswan, we visited the Philae Temple for an evening Sound and Light Extravaganza, as they over-lauded it. And a long desert drive to Abu Simbel, escorted part-way by three Egyptian army trucks – the soldiers all fully armed. One truck carried a heavy machine gun of some kind mounted on the back-bed.

The kids loved it and tried waving at the soldiers. One smiled and wiggled fingers in return, but the others were hawk-eyed and stony-faced – super alert.

'They know what you're like, Dad. They were expecting you.' Jo knows how to flatter me.

That was the furthest south we went.

After Aswan, it was a gentle downstream cruise back towards Luxor, calling at everywhere we'd skirted past on the way upstream. The Unfinished Obelisk. 'It looks like Broken Brendon,' my eleven-year-old commented. 'He's a fat 'orrible lad in my class.'

The temples at Edfu and Kom Ombo… a walk in the desert into the evening, and a campfire in the middle of nowhere. My three littlies were enthralled at the glory of a night sky never seen before. They loved Menhit for taking us there, as though she had personally arranged for the stars to exist, especially for my four blondes. 'We'll remember it *forever*,' Jo told her.

I felt ill, but smiled and let them have their time of adulation. *They're on holiday,* I told myself.

Another evening having a riotous laugh at my expense, but I was up for it. Menhit roped me in as the comedy turn on the quiz session, 'Which liner sank on its maiden voyage in 1912?' Even Brummie Brian knew that one.

'Were there any survivors? Yes or No?' Vacant Vera the pole dancer guessed that one right.

'You can name them?' she asked me, amid hoots of laughter from the post-meal drunks around a hundred tables.

Show me up all you like, I thought. *I'm on holiday.* 'Of course I can,' I told her in absolute self-assurance, 'Harland and Wolff.'

Menhit, Goddess of War, had no idea who built the Titanic, but she knew from reactions round the ballroom that I'd scored one there. The Lioness, She Who Massacres, was not pleased. Her eyes practically thundered at me behind an arctic smile. Her lips pouted fractionally. *That was the kiss of death,* I knew.

'I looked her up on Google again, Dad. Or her name, anyway. It means "Slaughterer". That means she kills everybody, doesn't it?'

'I think it means she does quite a bit of it; not necessarily *everyone*.' I was imagining who'd she'd pick on first.

The other passengers found our nightly jousting highly entertaining. The evidence was there for all to see – the photos on the entertainment board, posted at dawn each day. Every morning, a crowd gathered around the board, including our three little'uns, and I was getting all these comments about, 'Never forget that night…'

'How the hell did you manage that?'

'God, I've never laughed so much.'

'Can you stay an extra week or two, Effendi?'

I wasn't sure if Dad was the children's hero, or an embarrassment, most mornings, but an ice cream or much-desired trinket always bribed them round to smiles again.

'You're the star of the Show again,' Pervy Percy complained. He was the one who filmed the two belly

183

dancers every night. 'Apart from Batan and Raqisa, of course.'

The gallabiyah evening went especially well – I was nominated as the first one to do a routine, blindfolded and pretending to be a motorcyclist, and making all the right engine noises – except that Menhit told everyone else that I was sitting on a toilet. All good fun with the noises I was coming out with. Isn't it amazing how little girls can blush so darkly, though? When they're trying to disown you.

My evening was saved by my next obligatory event. Menhit came over to our table, her face a patchwork of flashing eyes and teeth. 'Your long desert gown, the gallabiyah, is perfect for a series of sketches I have arranged – two friends greeting each other – as pickpockets... or stockbrokers... lovers... doctors... You have to imagine how two such people might act when they meet; very exaggerated, and perform it together. Simple,' she grinned, and strode away with me sucked along in her wake. I sniffed to see if there was a waft of blood in her wake.

Brummie Brian and I threw ourselves into it, with imaginary stethoscopes, hands in each other's pockets, and pouting lips to die for. Kareem, our table waiter, claimed it was the best "interpretation" he'd ever seen. The applause when I went to see the photo board next morning seemed to support his opinion.

An evening drift along the river in a felucca... Tiny lights of a village that we swept past... Long trains of camels...

Back to Luxor. We'd been to the Amenhotep Temple on our first day – it seemed so long ago; and the Valley of the Kings, but we had one day left before the flight home, and two final events were on our itinerary.

184

The Colossi of Memnon was first. The two giant statues seemed to whistle when the wind was in the right direction. 'Like Whistler's Mother,' I stage-whispered, as Menhit gazed adoringly at the nearest one. She heard, didn't understand, but hated me more, just the same.

'Or Whistle down the Wind,' Jill suggested.

Then, to finish up, the coach took us round the hill to the Mortuary Temple of Hatshepsut, the Holy of Holies. 'Magnificent isn't the half of it,' I said. 'It's amazing.' Even from nearly a mile away in the coach park, in pale limestone, three storeys of columned glory stretched wider than the eyes could see along the foot of the mountain ridge.

'From here, you have to walk. We do not want this glory to be polluted with the likes of y— with coaches and cars.'

Which meant we had a long, baking hot walk in the noon-day heat of the desert. 'It's like running the gauntlet,' I said, 'at strolling speed,' as we delightedly went down the broad central avenue where all the souvenir stalls were lined up. My female four were enraptured at this massed shop-ertunity, anyway. Hundreds of visitors from many other tourist coaches were thronging that way with us – a lot of Germans and Chinese or Japanese among them, quite a few Scandinavians, too, judging by their appearance.

Accompanying us, Menhit abruptly stopped in the mass of tourists, blocking our way with outstretched arms. '*You* go *that* way.' She pointed to a side ramp. 'It is longer, but it will be much cooler in the shade for the young ladies. You may buy your souvenirs on the return, perhaps?'

185

I made as if to go round her, for the shorter walk, where the girls could look at all the goods on display and have a laugh and joke with the stall-holders.

'*No.*' Menhit insisted. '*You* go that way.'

'She's right; we can look on the way back,' Jill placated me, before I'd even thought about resisting further.

'Thank you, Menhit, Sajida.' I gave our beloved guide the biggest smile I could manage. She looked incredibly irritated. 'She's probably got an ambush set up for us.'

'She looks pregnant,' I ventured. 'Something she hasn't told us? Maybe Egyptian genius didn't stretch as far as birth control.'

'*Quiet, dear.*' It's an order when Jill says it in that tone.

'Well, it's not me who's—' I shut up.

The route she sent us along was about twice as far, but it *was* shaded and cooler, quieter, and much less frequented by stall-holders and tourists. We could see across to the central broadway where the crowd was jostling between the stalls. The girls could see Menhit two or three hundred yards away, slowly working her way among the tourists and stall-holders towards Hatshepsut's temple. Louise shouted and waved to her, and said she looked our way for a second. But she had her hands in her gallabiyah, and didn't wave back.

'Look. Can you see Menhit? Dad? Look, Dad, she just started shouting something and she looks mad about something.'

Yes, I could see her, too faint, too far away to hear anything. Wouldn't help. It'd be in Arabic.

'Everybody's backing away from—

'Wow… Wayyyy.'

The blinding flash wiped away the packed crowd right where Menhit was standing. Exactly from where she had taken up her position. In a micro-second, all those people ceased to exist. A massive shock. A vast gap in the world where so many people had been a moment earlier. Local Egyptians, stallholders and foreign tourists alike. Gone. God knows how many.

The blast hit us a second later. Not quite knocked over at that distance, but we were staggering back, shielding our faces. Did *she* do it? Or was she shouting a warning? Was it her? *Menhit – She who massacres.* She who'd deliberately sent us this way?

As the smoke rose, so fragments of people, concrete and souvenirs began spitting to the clay and limestone all around us like a chunky rain.

Something thunked onto my shoulder. It hadn't occurred to any of us, I think, that we might be hit by any pieces. Certainly not me. I looked down.

It was a finger. That finger. Leaving a splat and a little smear of blood, it slid down into the top pocket of my shirt, pointing up at me.

I know that finger. I know you well, with your emerald-painted nail, and a silver scar down the back of you. Menhit – Goddess of War. The times when she had stared at me when I irritated her. And that long finger had, on its own, pointed at me, so accusingly, before it crooked to order me to follow.

I had this really stupid thought. She liked my four blonde ladies, and she sent us this way? To protect them? *But she hated me; she was hardly going to protect me.*

Now. From my pocket, that all-commanding finger pointed at me still. *From right next to my heart.*

I felt a flutter.

MY BEST BET

'Gentlemen, gentlemen, gentlemen,' I attempted to bring the meeting to order, 'and Ladies – although you were already looking this way.' I gave the three ladies my finest beaming smile. It was genuine – they were the only reasonable souls in the room. *Probably the only ones with souls.* The eleven men had not an ounce of reason or charity between them, but they quietened and listened.

'You know I have to recommend the location for the collection compound, smelter and port. And the road and rail network down from the mining area.' *It's not a huge project as such enterprises go, but I've had so much trouble with this lot – everywhere round here is untouchably sacred, it appears.*

'I have been six months carrying out this task. It is my only role here. I do not have any say in quantities of ore to be extracted, and especially not whether or not the mining will commence. Such decisions are for the state authorities, the federal government and Rare Earths Dot Com. I merely survey possible sites, sketch out possible layouts, and make a recommendation on which one they might choose. They aren't totally bothered which site – they will largely take my word for it, bearing in mind all of your inputs. I imagine they will make a lot of money – shared between the various interested groups, including yourselves as Elders of the Original Peoples here.'

That upset them: they all had their individual opinion about what they were and what they represented. But I raised my hands to shush them, and, unusually, it worked. 'You and your peoples will become rich from this development.'

'It will not happen.'

'It must not.'

'It will. It has been inevitable since the discovery of several deposits of rare earth ores – notably praseodymium, cerium, lanthanum, neodymium, samarium, and gadolinium. There is, as we have many times discussed,' *if you can call such occasions discussions,* 'no way the powers that abound hereabouts will leave such essential and valuable wealth in the ground – especially on an uninhabited plateau that is frozen solid for half the year.' That brought them to their feet. All standing and demanding, putting me right, for the five hundredth time of late. I'm sure they dress up in their traditional – tribal – whatever – apparel for these events with me. It doesn't impress me – I see them on the streets, in the shops and bars and protesting at the mine sites, and they wear jeans, long-johns, micropore vests, shirts and Tog 99 Waterproofs. They drink – lots – swear like brass goblins, and their crime rate is way over the average. But they talk at me like they're custodians for the gods, Manitou and Star Wars' Force rolled into one.

'Gentlemen, Ladies. There *will* be a mining complex, with roads and rail lines down to the port, where there *will* be a collection area. Plus the first-smelter plant where the ores will be crushed-out and first-refined before being exported out of state to the Lower Forty-eight States. There, they will undergo full refining and shaping into bars for onward sale to manufacturers.' It's a relatively small quantity – one thousand tons of crude ore a week. One ship, carrying a

190

hundred metric tons of semi-refined product. Not huge amounts.'

Except the local tribes keep deciding that this was their ancestral homeland... their traditional place of prayer... the ancient playground of their gods... their forefathers' cemetery... the spiritual home of the animals... Something they invented in Mad Myran's bar the previous Friday night. Everywhere I surveyed and proposed, I was confronted with a whole list of objections.

'People!' *Get them back to order,* 'You know I have to make the recommendation by the end of the month—'
I had to pause for the howls of hatred and protest. They just didn't want any development anywhere on their land – not the mining, the roads or rail links, the smelters, the waste dumps, the water pollution, the air pollution, the jetties, or the frequent ship visits. Every single aspect of the development proposal was a real and present danger to their way of life, their heritage, their future, their beliefs...

'Oh, for Lord Pity's sake, people, I've bent over backwards, forwards and sideways, and accommodated everything you want. I now have to recommend. I've no choice, it's my job. I'm recommending the last one. It's no better or worse than the others, but it's uppermost in my mind; the arguments for and against it are no more compelling than for any of the other sites you turned down. This will happen. It's fed-owned land. It *will* happen.'

'You will be cursed forever.'

'That's not very nice of you, Aanjij.' She's one of the more moderate members of the meeting. I was hoping the men had been searched or scanned for

191

weapons as they came in, but maybe the three ladies, as well.

'We will save you from yourself.'

'We shall curse you to the nature around you...'

'Tell the spirits of your evil... '

'Yes, okay, you do that. But this *will* happen. I'm only the one who recommends on its location – the project will commence. I can give you a list of the people who do make the big decisions, if you want to target them accurately?'

They seemed to think I was being flippant, but such a list would have been easy to scribble out – the top chairmen, ladies, directors, owners, governors... around twenty with real influence.

On the snow-crusted grass outside my hotel room, all night, they were chanting and singing... couple of them taking turns to dance – the music was appalling. Smoking – twigs and leaves, and something rolled up that they passed round. Communicating with the spirits of the wildlife around here... informing them of my role in the incursion on their lands... the destruction I proposed.

'That's hardly fair,' I protested when I took out a trolley of coffee, cocoa and candy bars to keep them warm, and give me a rest. 'Funny how you pray in English, isn't it? They don't seem to be paying much attention to you?'

They weren't up to any such joviality, so I left them to it. 'I'll be crossing over Nuunatiak Sound in the morning, and catching a flight back to Anchorage from Tuntiliak Airfield. I'll be presenting my report the day after. Gentlemen, Ladies, that's it. I'm done.'

The orcas attacked the Arctic Queen two thirds across the sound. Crew were yelling orders and general panicky stuff and saying they'd heard of such attacks... Four of the huge beasts... then six... determined rams at the hull. Captain put his foot down or whatever they do. They were hitting at the rear... stern... One leapt up high, crashed onto the top deck, took the mast out – probably radio gone; maybe radar, too. Sheer panic then, except maybe me – I knew they were after me – never occurred to me to sacrifice myself and jump overboard. Me and the captain didn't lose it: he kept going. Must have been fifty of them – mass of raging water, spray, black and white masses... engine roaring and shuddering, cutting out... Captain managing to restart with increasing difficulty.

Other passengers shrieking about *killer* whales, and screaming and wide-eyed as well as mouthed; huddled below decks, but getting sprayed with water and splinters, just the same. Crew were mostly down there with them – nothing else they could do – not yet... hundred yards or more to go, the motor cut again, wouldn't restart.

The orcas getting frenzied, on top of each other to get at the vessel. Spray higher than the boat... getting in each other's' way, less effective in their attack.

She was holed, lower in the water, the decking wrecked and splintered, rails down, aft-cabin smashed. Four crew, faces drawn, struggling to the bow, dragging the mooring lines, to be ready if we ever made it to shore... Seeing a small cluster on the jetty, watching as though seeing an inevitable disaster – forty-plus deaths – loss of the only ferry along the sound.

Two of the black and white beasts came crashing onto the deck. So vast close up. Thrashing insanely; such power. Huge white teeth grinning as the damned things flailed and forced across the main deck. Beady-eyed, fixed on their victim. I'm sure it was me they were focused on. Just me – the others merely happened to be in the way. A group of the orcas was even pushing, ramming together on the port side... almost rolled her over; seemed so organised. Leaping out, one got tangled in the stays and went wild... that nearly sank her...

The motor re-started at the tenth push... loud and cranking... must have battered the prop... hardly any forward movement from her.

Even into the shallows, they followed... more and more splashing... almost frantic to sink her.

We were coming into the quay – crippled now, a heavy list to starboard, down at the stern. Barely any headway, as she swirled around in an eddy of raging whales

Throwing the line... and again... again... caught by willing, clutching hands... hauling us in... cheers from the crowd that had gathered in horror... waving and shouting in relief and gladness

God! That had to be the worst-ever voyage any vessel ever undertook... and remained afloat with master, crew and passengers all surviving. I think.

I never pray for anything, except then, as we were getting secured... on my knees for a moment of thanks.

'The Arctic Queen's a gallant craft, alright...'

'Should be refloatable...'

'Need a drink tonight...'

Gathering on the quayside as the Arctic Queen settled, top deck awash, everyone who'd been aboard was in deep shock – whether silent and sick, or arm-wavingly loud – and many were declaring their need for ale, and much that was considerably stranger.

'She was gallant, alright, but I'll never take a craft of that size across open water again.'

'Them buggers definitely had it in for us.'

For me. Fortunately, I'll be heading out by air in an hour or so… The Cessna 206 is the quickest way of getting back to Anchorage, and the orcas won't be able to get at me.

The taxi was waiting, though the driver hadn't expected me to survive as far as the shore; or be prepared to fly so soon after such an experience. He was full of chat about it, what he'd seen, how determined they'd seemed, 'Want to get away soon as, do you?

Half a mile, at most, and we were driving alongside the little airport's open field– it didn't even warrant a fence around it – towards the single building. 'What's that on the runway?'

He looked. 'Snow geese. Never seen so many together. They use scarers to keep them away.' Jerking the wheel as he drifted onto the verge, 'Like wriggling snow, aren't they?'

'Must be a thousand of them.'

'I know they get big flocks, but this… See'em all? Gathered round the Cessna, over the there. That your flight, is it?'

'They don't do kamikaze attacks on light aircraft, do they?'

He laughed, 'Never heard of it. Brought a few down, by accident, though. Why?'

'They seem to be gathering up on the runway…'

He looked… 'So they are. Don't worry about it: Jeppo wouldn't even try to take off through a flock like that. Too dense.'

That leaves me a mite desperate. 'I really need to be at a meeting in Anchorage. How long would the drive be? By road? Like in a taxi?'

'Me, you mean? There's not a road, as such, all the way. It's tracks that link adjoining spreads.'

'You've been?'

'I have. Not many have. It'd be a fourteen-hour drive... two-days.'

'Are you up for it? Share the driving? Travel all night?'

'Not too sure about that, Sir—'

'I'll pay double.'

'Don't think so... there's been reports this morning of large concentrations local wildlife through that area. Caribou, bears and the like been seen along the road at several points.'

All day, there have been reports coming in on unusual animal concentrations. Masses of different species are congregating around the airport and outlying roads.

By late afternoon, it appears that the wildlife is gathering in increasing variety and numbers even closer to the outskirts of Tuntiliak.

After a whole day of increasingly alarming such reports, I'm thinking that my best bet is to go to the edge of town with my report, and wave it for all to see. Then, perhaps, I should give a short explanation, like, 'This is what you're after, not me,' pour gasoline all over it, and put a match to it.

I'm counting on them realising what I'm doing, and being understanding with me.

I just hope that wolves are reasonable creatures.

OOPS

'Get here asap, Doctor Bealard. We'll have a patrol car at the Bar Lane layby past the Five-Way Island, and escort you to the site under a blue light. But make it there fast, Doc. It sounds pretty desperate from the scene.'

'Bar Lane layby? the west side of the Island? I should be there in ten minutes – car's all ready. Leaving now.'

I touched Record, and did a swift log, '10.30 p.m. Called out to attend a Road Traffic Collision on the motorway – A big, serious one, from the officer's description. Two lorries, perhaps three cars. The controller's stressing how serious it is, four casualties they know of already, one critical, and probably more trapped in a vehicle underneath an artic. All foam-blanketed because fuel's leaking.' Touch the red button to sign off – I like to have my own log of incidents, as well as their recordings.

Hi ho – I'm on rota till midnight, but it's only the second call-out this week. Quick check the bags are in my car. The First Call Doctor is already out at a house fire out of area, so it's me.

It's going through my mind as I'm driving off – drips, saline, full bloods… splints, braces, pain-killers… So vital to get to them quickly… And get some sleep before I have to be back on the road in the morning. Long day tomorrow.

197

Well, we were sitting there in the Underhill layby while the Green Wagon Nightcafe was closing up. Keeping an eye on the truckers for any erratic or suspicious behaviour – boozers or smugglers, our main targets. Boring, boring, boring. 'Aye aye, Sarge, we've got one coming up the rear. He's doing well over forty.'

'Let's have him,' Sarge says, and I flick the blue on and he swings her out. This feller's going to keep going. 'Think you can outrun us, huh? Belt up tight, PC.' And he pedalled it, screwed her across the carriageway and cut this guy up. Lights everywhere and we're waving and he decides to pull up before we get to the Five Ways…

'Offence Number Two, Sarge,' I mention. 'Halting a vehicle on the carriageway in a dangerous or unsafe manner.'

He's just sitting there when we get out and order him out. He never moved. 'So, he's being awkward, is he?' Sarge says, 'Cover him while I go close.'

So we both had our tasers out and ready, and Sarge goes in, ordering him out and against the vehicle. So out he gets, all mouth and attitude, waving his hands round and shouting the odds and won't shut his face. 'Shut up, you old git. Sir.' I ordered him.

'Do as ordered. Turn and put your hands on the car.' Sarge ordered him again. We don't do three repeats.

But he kept protesting, 'But I have to be at Five Ways—'

'He sounds drunk to me, Constable.'

'You're in no kind of calm mood to be safe on the Queen's Highway,' I told him.

'Listen to me—'

'No. You listen to us, Sir.'

'But I'm needed—'

'Shut up and get against the vehicle.'

'I've been called—'

I went in closer, taser pointed and ready. That'd calm him down. Quell him if he tried to make a dash for it, or attacked the sergeant.

He says, 'Calm down yourself, young man; it's you who's getting aeriated, not me,' Still waving his arms round. He moved. Going to reach into the car. Or going for the sergeant. So I'm shouting my warning at him to calm down, and Sarge lets him have it with his taze; so I do as well, to make sure. He's screaming and on the floor and jerking all round and we kept'em on just a few seconds longer, to make sure he stayed down. 'Huh, Calling you "Young Man", eh, Amanda? His eyesight's not too good, eh? Book him for that as well.'

'Dump his car on the grass and leave it here. Get him in the back and down the nick – Lord Street Station'll be fine for one night. Central's busy. He can pay a visit to the magistrate at nine in the morning. Add resisting arrest to the count.'

 And finally on the Midday News… A doctor who was due to be awarded the George Cross at Buckingham Palace this morning appears to have been kidnapped on his way to an emergency callout last night. Dr John Bealard was to have been given the honour in recognition of his conspicuous courage in circumstances of extreme danger.

On four occasions he has risked his life treating the injured in hazardous situations. Over the past three years, these have included being under fire from the gunmen who took hostages at the London siege last summer; treating three people trapped in the Islington block of flats inferno; and aiding injured shoppers who had taken refuge in the Dog and Partridge public house during the East End riots two years ago.

Since moving to the Midlands, he was also inside the Waldene Textiles factory after the first collapse during demolition work, treating a work crew. He was the only survivor of the subsequent complete collapse of the factory. Aged seventy-one, he has also been known for his outspoken views on a number of issues.

He is thought to have been forced off the road and kidnapped whilst travelling to a major traffic incident on the motorway, in which five people are known to have died at the scene. His car has been found, looted of his medical bags which contained vital drugs and medical equipment.

The queen has asked to be kept informed of progress. More of this for our Midlands viewers in your local news after this broadcast.

'Sarge?'

'Amanda?' He looked up, still dozy, 'Get back here in bed. We got ages yet before anybody misses us.' He glanced across the sparse room that was provided at the Central Police HQ for officers requiring an overnighter. *Amanda looks bloody good,* he thought. *She'd look better back in here.*

'Sarge? I just had a call from Western Division about last night. They were expecting the emergency doctor to meet them at the Bar Lane layby for that motorway pile up. They're not happy about him – three people died at the scene when he might well have saved'em.' She sniffed and tried to pull her bra on one-handed. 'We were the other side of the Five-Ways Island till about twenty-three hundred hours, and I said we didn't see anything suspicious – no crash or forcing off the road.'

200

'No, nothing like that, Amanda, my dear little WPC,' Sergeant Faibla sat up, pushing the bed covers away, 'it was just that old trouble-causer we dropped off at Lord Street nick at midnight. The one who was speeding and mouthing off. Had to taze him quiet, didn't we? I expect they'll have called the local on-call doctor out for him this morning.'

'Yeah, looked a bit sicky, dinne?'

'I've no idea, I let you and PC Jackson deal with him once we got there. Walked didn't he? That's fit enough. Okay, so he didn't exactly walk,' Sergeant Faibla conceded, 'but he was breathing, wasn't he?'

Amanda was still struggling to untangle her black tights, paying as much attention as she usually did to anything that wasn't in bed. 'Recharged your T26, have you, Sarge?'

'I love it when you talk dirty like that, Girl.'

'Think we should go round and fill in the paperwork on him, when we get dressed, eh?'

'Maybe. In a bit. Stick the telly on, Amanda; see if there's anything on the news...'

SATNAV SADIE

'At last.' I felt like relaxing after the long flight from England. The Midland Tourist Park, in the suburbs of Perth, Western Australia was a convenient holiday chalet park for a week's stay, the first leg of a month-long holiday Down Under.

The first day there, we slept until noon, picked up the rental car, a crate of ale and a Chinese takeaway.

Day two, we headed for the Nambung National Park, around 150 miles north of Perth, as the car wanders. Through Perth and onto Route 60, through Yanchep National Park. Easy driving at the low maximum speed they permitted here – it's like you're expecting a speeding snail to come hurtling past you. An age of increasingly hot, rising sun, semi-desert, distant sea views on occasion, rock-ridged mountain crests. A couple of kangaroos bounding across the road... three that hadn't made it.

'I wonder how long we've been driving,' Penny addressed no-one in particular, i.e., me.

'You have been driving two hours.'

It was the SatNav. Jeez. Talk about shocked. We both stared at it in disbelief. 'It's listening to us...'

'Spying on us.'

'You have been driving two hours. You should take a break.'

That was genuinely a relief. 'It's automatically exercising its sense of social responsibility.'

'Turn left onto clickclickclick road.' It got rather tongue-tied when it came to the longer names.

**

At long last, we found Nambung National Park. Magnificent! The huge Pinnacles Desert was the site of hundreds of rock points and pillars scattered liberally across the blazing sun-lit landscape. Each rock tower was around twice the height of a person. Some tall and thin, some shorter, and pointed. There was a made-up road winding through the parkland, and we stopped a dozen or more times to wander around, take photos and examine the rocks close up, not straying too far from the car in that sandwich-baking heat.

It was a really zig-zagging route around the area, and the SatNav was getting confused by the time we left the park, spinning round like your first time in Ann Summers. We headed for the coast at Hangover Bay to make our way back to our temporary home at the Midland Tourist Park

'Do not go on the bridge if you cannot see the highway,' it told us.

'Eh? What's that? In case of floods?'

'Have you checked the fuel?'

'What the nanny-nav is this?'

'You should check the water.'

'Does the windshield need to be cleaned?'

It was every ten minutes that it piped up with something new. Can't Aussie drivers think of such things for themselves?

'You have been driving for eight hours without a break...'

'No, I haven't.'

'Stop at the clickclickclick...'

'You should take a break now... for at least one hour...'

'How do you turn her off?' It didn't have anything to say for five minutes after Penny suggested that.

'*You should…*

'*Keep on this road until you come to the clickclickclick.*'

The little map on the screen started spinning round again. 'She's got lost,' Penny decided.

'She's back in Ann Summers.'

She regained herself, with a big brown arrow pointing back the way we'd come.

'Wonderful,' I decided. 'Just what I need.'

She dropped off the windshield and landed under the brake pedal. Again.

Then she decided, '*Battery is depleted. Closing down.*' And turned the screen to blank for several minutes while she recovered from the shock of my language – I'm fluent in Oscenità.

The shortcut she was taking us on was getting narrower… and narrower. 'Ah, a galvanised steel gate into a dried-out field.' That was the end of that road.

'*Turn around when possible.*' We had to reverse out, almost half a mile to the next field gateway for a turn. That was what you might call the Effing Time.

Sometime during the reversing process, she decided to adopt the voice of an American lady, called Bonnie.

Abruptly, she mistakenly realised that we wanted to go to Perth, Scotland, instead of the Perth fifty miles away in Western Australia.

'*Your journey involves a ferry. Continue?*'

**

Half a mile south of Joondalup, the arrow spun round ninety degrees. *"Turn around when possible"*. So we did. But she said the same thing on the alternative road out of Joondalup. And the same again on the third option, which only left the one we'd originally come along. We spun round and took the route we'd originally been aiming for.

205

A couple of miles further, the screen rotated for two minutes and settled for *that* direction after all.

'Take the next left... along Clickclickclick Road.'

I signalled, turned. 'Urghhhh!!!' I was facing straight into four lanes of traffic lined up at the lights, aiming directly at me. A swift reverse and rear-wheel skid got us out of there just as the lights changed.

**

I couldn't tell the rental car guy what had happened to SatNav Sadie, as we called her. 'She must have been stolen,' we said, 'kidnapped.' I gave him the cash, rather than claim on the insurance.

He must have suspected the truth, but it had been exceedingly satisfying to place her carefully under the front offside wheel and drive over her. We each did it twice, down some back road she'd taken us down just outside Gidgegannup.

'You hear that?' I said, as I dropped the crushed remnants into a bin.

'What?'

'She's still squawking that it's me who's gone wrong somewhere.'

TAKE THESE CHAINS

'Well, if you must know,' They always wanted to know everything straight away. No settling first. 'I'd been doing my shopping; got back to my car with Delilah…'

'At last,' I says. 'Shopping all completed. That's it for this week, old girl. Come on, let's get it all loaded in the back.' Lord, I felt like I was chained to all my carrier bags of various shapes, sizes and weights. 'Get this lot put away, eh?'

'Hruff.' Tail clouting my leg.

'I'm glad you agree, Delilah. And a double mug of tea for me as soon as we get home; and Treet-a-Pooch for you, eh? Hello, what's this? Somebody at the car?'

Just what I need. A girl – she's a quarter my age, so she's a girl – has chained herself to the back of my car. And she's got an awful lot to say to me and everybody else who'll listen.

Most won't listen. They stop for a moment, tell her she's batty, and wander off. She was protesting about something. It wasn't clear what – didn't sound too rational to me. 'Alright, Duck,' I said, 'But I need to put all my shopping down and get home and put my feet up.'

'You stupid old git.' She started effing and blinding when I tried to put my shopping in the car, and get Delilah in there as well, and see how she'd fixed the chain. She was fighting me off, screeching. Determined to confront someone, some issue or other – personal, not a national issue like women's rights or gays for all. No… it sounded like trouble with her boyfriend, who might have been called Benny Fitz – that or her social payments weren't up to scratch. Or Benny was squandering them.

207

Whichever, she was protesting about it, and was determined to tell everybody.

'We could move the chain to a lamppost or the One Way sign,' I offered. 'I'll do it, if you like.'

Came at me all scratches and kicks, she did. Course, Delilah defended me – backed off and barked once; cowered a bit. So I was all scratched-up and got a head wound in the first round. Stone me! I'm seventy-five and not here to take violence and abuse from some teenage nutcase.

So I spent five minutes picking my shopping up whilst under attack and trying to retreat. She kicked and spat at me the whole time. 'Interfering effing old git...' she was going on. I wished I hadn't bought so much – but it was all essential stuff; just such a bind not being able to get it all into my car straight away.

'It's you who's interfering,' I told her. 'It's my car, young lady.' I stepped away, out of range and got my old Nokia out and called 999.

They told me to call 911.

'We'll get back to you,' they said.

They didn't.

I called them again and they said, 'If no-one has been harmed or is at risk of harm, then it is not an emergency.' They cut the call.

I rang back.

'Are you causing a breach of the peace? We've had a call about a disturbance.'

'Does peeing myself in the street count as a breach of the peace?' I asked. 'I'm getting a mite desperate.' She rang off.

I called 999 again, but the police were busy.

'Yes,' I said. 'In their car outside the chippy on Walton St. Him and her on the back seat. Sharing their vinegar, I bet.' So they cut that call, as well.

I rang 911 again.

I think they were expecting me. 'Well sir, you go and be a good sir. Have a nice cup of tea and sit down, and please don't block this line again. And stop wasting our time, eh, sir?' Went dead. Like her.

By then I was in the Potted Cat, the café just off High Street, and the two ladies looked at me, 'You ought to go in the toilet and clean that nasty cut and all those scratches.'

'We'll make a pot of tea for one, and a water-bowl for your hairy friend.'

'Tie her lead to the corner table and leave your shopping bags; we'll keep an eye on them. Month's shopping, is it?'

So I did, and I was a bit shaken up and needed the sit down and the cuppa, and rang my daughter to fetch me – she was shopping somewhere along the road. Not answering, though; so I left a message.

But after half an hour she hadn't got back to me and I was feeling better, so I thought I'd go back and see if the ratty girl was still there. It was too cold to stay out all night. Besides, the café shuts at six-thirty.

The door-bell dinged just as I was finishing my drink, and this policeman came in, up to the counter for a few words, nodding in my direction, 'What?' I ruffed Delilah's ears. 'We haven't been a nuisance or anything in here.'

But he came over, 'Where did you sustain your injuries?'

'On my head,' I told him.

209

'There's no need to be like that, Sir. Merely doing my job. I'm going to have to ask you to go with me.'

'Yes, they said that in Germany in 1940 when they carted everybody off to the concentration camps. But I can't go with you, I'm waiting for my daughter.'

He said, 'You're not Jewish.

And I said, 'You're a Zion denier, are you? You don't know if I'm Jewish, and what's that got to do with it, anyway? The Nazis took gypsies, homosexuals and political agitators into the camps as well as Jews.'

'You aren't—'

'Stop there, officer, before you accuse me of all sorts of irrelevant things. You'll have to arrest me and carry me because I'm going nowhere with you, not voluntarily. And anyway, I'm going nowhere with a stranger who hasn't even shown me any ID.'

'Very well, Sir, I'm arresting you—'

'On what charge?'

'Breach of the peace and suspected involvement in a murder.'

That got my attention a bit more. It also confused me: 'I haven't killed anyone today, as far as I recall,' I told him. 'Or ever before, for that matter. It was very peaceful in here until you jackbooted your way in. Isn't that right?' I appealed to all the rest of the coffee and cake crowd in there.

He was pulling at me to go with him, but I insisted he formally arrest me, using the correct wording and showing me his warrant card. And do it properly, in front of a dozen witnesses.

'I want Mirandising,' I told him.

'You're in the wrong country for that, Sir. You have the right to remain silent…'

210

'So what's this all about?' But he wouldn't say, and he said I'd have to leave Delilah and all my shopping there.

'All of it? That's practically my life savings invested in that lot.'

That was just as two more police arrived; a young feller and a woman. Both fresh-faced and eager. They practically carried me outside to their car. First-Fuzz told them to inspect my shopping. I said they couldn't do that without a search warrant and he shoved me against the car and frisked me. That's what they call it when they want to feel you up on the sly.

Then when the other two came out they handcuffed me! And stuffed me in the back of a van that they sent for. That really cracked my shin and hit the side of my head when I fell onto the metal panelling. My glasses came off and my hearing aid stopped working and one got in with me and she had her foot on me. 'To restrain you, Sir.' So I was laid out on the floor while we went off to somewhere with a courtyard – modern grey-stone and brick place.

They pulled me out and took me up a load of iron-grid steps, then down lots of stairs and locked me in a little cell room. Still with handcuffs, no glasses or hearing aid, and dying for a pee again.

Softening me up for a confession – Yes, I killed JFK… and the Archduke Ferdinand. *Maybe they think I was the third Moors Murderer?*

It was excruciatingly uncomfortable, so I went to the little peep-hole in the door and shouted that I needed a pee, 'Or I'll have to do it here.'

Some yob in uniform came up and said, 'A man's got to do what a man's got to do.' So I did.

It was another half-hour or so before they sent somebody in, all sniggers and smirks and told me to mop up the pee.

'I can't,' I told her, 'it's all in my right shoe. And I'm concussed from the head-bashing and kicking I got in your van. Not to mention, I'm far too upset and distracted by the discomfort and smell. I haven't had a phone call. I haven't seen a solicitor, nor seen my daughter. Plus, my insulin dose is overdue and I'm feeling hypo. I've got the trembles, heart flutter and sweating. You're blurred. I can't see as far as the floor; and I'm wearing handcuffs.

'And you've made me miss Emmerdale.'

She stormed out in the middle of me saying I hadn't got my oxybutynin pills – or my fenofibrate, flecainide, warfarin, atorvastatin, bisoprolol, inhaler, sumatriptan and all the others. 'And I need to go for a Number Two as well. I'm seventy-five,' I called after her, 'see how you manage, if you're lucky enough to survive that long with your attitude.' They'll probably charge me with threatening the life of a police officer, having said that.

They took their time, and tried to bully me more and more, with all their demands and pushing me about and wanting me to tell them all about the girl I'd chained to the back of a car and murdered.

Until my daughter arrived and put a stop to it all. She's a lawyer and knows all the rules. Inhumane treatment… police brutality… unfounded charges… Serious over-use of restraints against a frail old pensioner… a widower...

So they had to let me shower and go to the toilet properly. I hate showers, but they hadn't got a bath. Cleanish clothes, and it had been five hours in custody without being offered a drink or any food. Deprived of my medications; no doctor when I had requested one.

212

They still didn't really believe there was anything up with me, and kept going on about me fighting with this girl and tying her up with a chain and driving away with her dragging behind. 'Ripped to shreds, she is – no skin or clothes left... just raw meat.'

That conjured up a not-nice vision, 'It was her attitude that was raw... and roar,' I told them. 'Anyway, I was in the café all the time.'

'Racist killing was it?'

'Eh?'

'The girl, she was mixed race, wasn't she?' Sounding dead sarcastic and patronising. I can do without you.

'She was? I never noticed – she was bright red in temper, was all I saw.' I told them that, and they said that proved it was a racist hate crime if I carried out murders so routinely that I didn't even notice what colour someone was.

'Eh?' I had to wonder about the logic of that.

So my daughter, Angelica, was recording all this in the interview room on her iThing, getting on-line and checking up on some legal point. How they do, you know, these youngsters.

Big smile, suddenly. She can really turn on the smile, asking so sweetly if they'd seen the latest up-story on Facebook... YouTube and Twitter. Something on her mobile, anyway.

'Huh? Grunt, grunt. Wha'?' Furrowed brows and armpit-scratching.

I was famous. Three different people had mobile-filmed my altercation with the girl, and up-loaded it all. She was a bit tanned, I suppose. And it was clear that she was having a nasty-tempered go at me. One of the nosy sods had it videoed from before I even got there, and had been streaming it live – her all mouth and protests about some boyfriend who treated her badly.

She even knocked me over once and kicked me… and scratched me… and I'd fled with my shopping. It was all there.

Less than a minute after I'd tottered off, she was checking the car, and the reg plate, and moving her chain to the one behind mine – same colour. Boyfriend turns up. There's a big row; she's all mouth and waving again, going for him, and hitting at him with the chain and he jumps in and drives off while she's still ranting and bashing at the driver's door and glass, all shrieks and spitting.

Whipped off her feet, still raging at him. Dragged off behind him at high speed; hand-brake U-turn round the bollards. She rolled like a pendulum across the road, and he came hurtling back with her still attached by that chain – rolling and bumping and all bloodied.

He did it twice more. Right round the war memorial up the top of the street. There was blood and bits everywhere.

'Alright? So now you know why the High Street was closed for cleaning… Now then, whose round is it?'

THE BRASS KETTLE DINER

Two minutes in the ladies' restroom to check for any remaining oil smudges across my cheeks, run my fingers through my hair and tie it back, then it's out to face the diner crowd.

Tail-gate! That place was a whole nother sperience. I was hit by the heat – hot nuff to bake a bagel. Stifling, and over-aromatic from burned hash-browns. Powed back on my fanny by music filling the air almost as much as the flies. They swarmed in scores, slaughtering themselves on the UV zappers on every wall. *Whoa. This place is something else – all git out with flies and folk, food smells and heat; and a whole wagon-full of zapping, yacking and yelling from all quarters.*

Scarce any surprise I'm sounding more Texan than the frigging locals after two years cruising the Fourth Quarter of the US – the south-West. Think Houston to LA – which is fifty percent Texas. Long way from home for a Mid-West gal. I got too much baggage building up out there, so I got out.

And this p.m, I find myself unwillingly here with a blown rubber, and I'm developing a real deep feel of foreboding as I'm looking round this garbage pit of a diner with a truck park.

Six young fellers sitting by the window grills, keeping eyes on their three big-o pickups outside, with a deer slung up in the back of each, dripping blood that's trickled down the runnels and pooled under the rifle chest where the flies already were gorging themselves like hogs on high days. All grins and beers – the guys, not the flies.

215

A jabbering trio of uniformed girls blocked the aisle when I attempted the reach the bar. They were from Arcade Heroes out yonder, across the way, with voices shrill as bats in flight and never hearing a word the others said. Or realising anybody wanted to get past them. *Oh, shit, ladies, get out my way* – but I went round the other side of the tables instead of saying anything. *No mood for a fight after the day I just had rolling eighteen wheels long the highway.*

Two servers up near the serving bar were chattering away and ignoring the queue and the smoking dishes on top of the range.

Jeez, the hot fat'n'food smell in this place! Stinging my eyes like prickle-pines. But what the heck? Where else you gon go? So I joined the back of the queue.

Three guys on the table next to where I stood were vets from Vietnam, their caps as faded as their thoughts of hero days when friends were killed and enemies fried. You can tell just from looking at'em. One of them's wife had a drawl that spread out a single word for three seconds or more. But they listened to her, cos she's bigger than them, and she'll be getting the check.

Yacking Grandpaw in the corner with a four-year old on happy pills; him with his clackers dancing and spinning around his wrist, and the kid agog at his dexterity and occasional wrist-rapping misjudgement with the solid-steel clacking balls. But more agog with his disintegrating pizza than grandpaw's toy.

Six feet tall and six around, the stetsoned woman in the corner booth took in the orders from the bar-queue and the table-server girls, and bellowed them out in staccato barks to the kitchen staff ten feet behind her. An unseen receiver in the blue-haze-filled Hole of Tucson repeated them all at the top of his voice, probably much to the detriment of his vocal cords in that atmosphere.

Jeez – the racket in here is like having a dozen Dodge Challengers on the starting grid. The thick stink of burned fat… the packs of yacking kids stuffing their mouths full round every table.

Nother passel o' kids screeched and squealed all over a pair of tables close to the drinks machines – ten or a dozen of them aged around three to eight. Like I'd know kids' ages. All ablaze with excitement and chatter and telling their moms and pops and grandies 'bout ener-thang and ever'thang – as they say round these parts. Climbing over the tables and food, and knocking the drinks over. Hysterical OTT greetings as a pack of new good ole buddies appeared through the doors at the back – the kids as bad as the adults. In they came, erupting across a pair of other tables as well.

Don't matter, I ain't heading anywhere near that lot. Cacophonous place this is. Lemme outa here.

Standing there in the queue, I was feeling less and less agreeable with the idea of sitting down amid this excerpt from a Longhorns home game. After a day on the road sitting down, I was thinking that maybe a take-out appeals more than kamikaze attacks by a trillion flies, plus deadly assaults by the reek of food from Mexico and Italy, as well as New York and LA.

Jeez, there must be another place close by – it'll drive me to Bakersfield if I have to stay in here another minute.

'Jeet yet?' She appeared next to me, and drawled through the chewing gum, so bored with the job and her life she might as well join the army.

'Would I be stood here if I'd eaten a'ready?'

'Kay. Sit down, Lady. Find a table. Be with ya soon.'

The way out was blocked with a new gang of suicidal would-be diners, and there warnt no other exit. So I found a seat in the jostling mass and parked myself, more in feelings of fear and doom than hope and hunger. Mostly craving a coupla beers to wash down the day I'd had – three-fifty miles on the Interstate since six a.m.

Windshield full of flies all day, now I got grilled-over and greased-up windows I can scarcely even see for the inch-deep flies that's thronging all over'em. The yackering kids and yelling staff didn't help. Nor the blasting music that twanged and swirled and knurled in a Tex-Mex mix of plastic cactus songs and senoritas by the score. Sometimes, sure. But after the day I had, it did my head in. *This place is more manic than the I - 95 at Newark.*

Six inches above my head, a yell like a road-smash. Another order was shrieked across the room and repeated back in a bellowing roar from Stetson in the Booth; and then picked up by Hazy Joe in the Kitchen. And somebody else in there just had to yell it back to confirm it. *Oh shoot. All this cos of a flat tire.*

'You ready to order?' A spotty young server appeared after I spent twenty minutes trying to wave at him, catch his eye – *best not do my ear-splitter whistle*, I reckoned. But he'd been content just gazing round like something with hoofs. Me craving a drink of Dos Equis beer, and he craving oblivion by the looks of him. *Yer already halfway there*, I thought.

'I been ready a day or more,' I said.

He pulled a face. 'Gee, you're a funny gal. So what's y' dope on a dish, Trucky?'

I told him, 'Chicken, Dixie-style. *Servy.*'

218

'With all the fixings?'

I nodded, 'Coupla beers'd be good.' He went. Nother interregnum of waiting, flies still plastering themselves round the windows and screens, and on the displays of cakes and cookies that stood on the bar. The pile of un-bussed dishes at the other end of my table was growing as some mouthy kids dumped their dishes on me. I felt like pushing'em off onto the floor. But I'm not the attention-seeking kind. Not today.

Just over yonder, by the washrooms, there's this upper-teen with greasy hair she's never *ever* washed; spots, and heavy glasses and heavier teeth. She's up on her feet and ordering mom around... 'You can't have that... If you order that I'm not sitting with you. Sit *there*, Mom.' She never stops. 'I'll decide. I'll order for you, mom.'

Grandpaw with the clackers around his wrist has given up his efforts to teach the kid to twist his wrist and break it with the pair of steel balls. So now he's happy enough to clack his balls at a rate of knots, splitting the air with incessant cracks and cackles and yelps and hooping hollers and plastic teeth on the verge of taking a tumble in the direction of the floor – Lord spare ener-thang that landed down there.

Crash! Squawk. A shriek that carried on and on. It was joined by another. A woman in a pink sun-top had tumped an over-filled dish from the hot-buffy bar, and narrowly missed the head of her kid, so they fed off each other's yelps and hysterics. They sobbed, and started to refill another dish to console them-fat-selves.

The Fifty High-Pitched Words Per Second Server Girl was coming at me, 'Howdy y'all. The Chicken Dixie's off. Chef's done y' Southern Prawns instead.

Here. That OK? Yeah, Right. One minute, I'll fetch y'coke.' She rattled it out in half a sec and was gone.

Coke? Me? Omigod what is this filthy dump I've landed in? Wrong food. Wrong drink. Come back Attica, all is forgiven.

I must have had *that* look on my face and opened my mouth to call after the rattle-mouthed server.

'Best y' don't do that, little lady.' A slow voice slid onto the seat opposite me. A real purt feller my age with shoulders wide as the hood of my truck. Big easy smile as he settled himself, 'Don't mind if I park my rig, do ya? Suzy-Fast don't take it good if you turn it down. Kin swap if you like. I had the last of the Dixie Chix; but I don't mind the prawns they do here.'

He smiled again and pushed his tray my way. 'She'll get y' drink right; ev'thang's coke to Suzy. They oughta bring a can o' fly and skeeter spray with ever' dish. Yer seein' the wildlife now at their minimum best. There's a ton or more per table in the summer heat.'

'We talking flies or kids?'

I ate his Chicken Dix and he consumed the prawns; and we sank a pair of Equis. 'Whad'a'ya'll doing here?' he said. 'Gal like you?'

'My rig's out back, the Freightliner Semi.'

'The 18-wheeler with a flat on the front? Ess-Dubya Trucking?'

'That's the one. I pulled a plank with coupla nails just down the road, so I gotta wait to get it changed. Company rules. Not allowed to change it on my own. So I'll have to wait till noon tomorrow when the mechanic comes out from Alapac. Whole day lost.' I jiggled my empty bottle, 'You want another?'

220

'Hell, no, not yet. Let's get y' tire fixed. Half an hour is all. It's only the front, not an inside rear. I'll give you a check to send on in, if it helps you keep straight with the company.'

Hey... Who's to argue with an offer like that? I was suddenly happy. 'Save me a day just hanging round here.' I take another look around the bedlam surrounds, and another at my uninvited guest who's looking at me with his easy smile.

'Yeah. Why not?' I says, cos he's – Hell, he's just my type, so what the heck?

So it took an hour, the two of us, me and Jess, and we talked on rigs, and roads we've known, and spoke of loads we've carried and places we've been, and he's going the other way come dawn. 'But back in here tomorrow night,' he said. 'It's where I'm based four nights a week. Got a regular room; cabin out the rear.'

When we get back inside, the music's changed to R&B and a Country mix with Mexican flair. The families with a million kids have gone, and it's the teen-tribe to the right of the bar, and the truckers all twenty-plus the left side and chewing the cud and there's a fight on TV soon with Marriaga fighting Stevenson in the Featherweight Champs. So we sit with the guys, and yell for José Luis to bring the beers, and we sink s'more Dos Equis.

Chimichangas are top of the late board, with fries on the side, with nachos and cheese. Dolores turns up behind the bar and gets a cheer, but I don't know why.

A dreamy eve, but we both need to be on the road by dawn, so I'm on my own in the sleeper cab of my rig in the parking lot.

Come five a.m. I'm up and filling my tank and on the road, all the way to Albanay to drop the 'tainer at MZ Cord's and collect another from round the block to bring back here to Tucson South.

I'm turned around by noon, then I got to have an hour's break before I'm back on the I - 105 and cruising down to The Brass Kettle Diner a mile to the south of Tucson Town. The parking lot's got a space reserved for me right out back, and I can use the facilities for free.

The neon sign that sags one side will beckon me in from a mile away, and I'll open the door, and the cool and fragrant air will wrap its caring cloak around me. Dolores'll be on the bar.

And Jess'll be there with his ice-blue eyes and big easy smile, and hands that can rip a tyre clean off its rim, he says. First one in'll save a seat and have the drinks all paid, and he'll tell me about his wife and kids – and I'll tear him apart if does do that. Cos before first light s'mornin, he told me he'd never wed, cos he'd never found a gal with half the nerve to drive a rig in reverse at twenty-five around the lot and into the shed where the fuel's stored. Like I did in the dark at five o'clock.

The game'll be on the TV and the guys'll be rooting for Tucson Sugar Skulls and I might have the nerve to yell for mine – Sioux Falls Storm. Hell, yeah, course I will.

'Y' never kept y' trap shut yet,' my old boss at Sioux City packing plant told me. Like it was Des Moines Public Library Tuesday noon.

'Jes competing with the hogs,' I always told him, looking at the guys in Maintenance.

'There's also a special on tonight on Medolo beer with fajitas and chillies and guacamol'. That's from seven till nine, same as the game. Tequila sunrise is on till midnight. And jus' maybe, Jess'll be on till dawn.

Yeah... I reckon maybe I'm coming to love that ol' place

...with all its flies and fast-talk staff

...and grandpaw's clackers

...and the upper teen with heavy teeth.

And Jess, the Wichita guy with the Kenworth W - nine-nine-zero semi with vertical stacks, who hangs around the Brass Kettle Diner and Bar, on the I - one-oh-five at Tucson South.

WAITING FOR THE GREEN MAN

'Oooff. Uff.' I toppled forward, staggering a bit off-balance. Stick out to stop myself falling.

I waited. Gertrude, my carer, started finger-writing on the palm of my hand as I turned in the direction of whatever had slammed into me. She's very good like that – always likes to keep me up-to-date with everything happening around me. It helps me to feel still attached to the world, not merely floating disembodied through it.

There I was, on the edge of the pavement, waiting to cross the road, when I was abruptly crashed into. I mean – when you have no vision at all – not even an odd stray beam of light – and are totally deaf, you can feel a wee bit cut off from the world. So being bashed about comes as something of a surprise. A shock, even. I just hadn't been expecting it. Took the wind out of me.

I was trying to figure it out from what Gertie wrote, but I got pushed again. I got cross: it felt deliberate, intended.

'A man is shouting that he's blind,' according to Gertie's swift hand-scrawling. 'He demands all-round attention from everyone on the street. He wants you to get out of his way. Very loud, he is.'

I've since been told that his white stick whirled round twice, flailing at me, before it caught me on the head. I felt that, alright; there's nothing wrong with my senses of touch, pain, and affrontedness.

Now, I'm not violent by nature, and I'm not vindictive or sadistic. However, this guy was asking for some natural justice. Really, he was. Even Gertie signed

225

so. But I'm not ill-tempered. My retraining has helped a lot.

I wasn't in the least tempted to paste him one on the end of his nose. That was largely because I couldn't tell where his nose was, how far away, or how tall he was. That sort of relevant factor.

'Duck.' Gertie wrote, and I felt her bend down.

Just as I was wondering what tonight's meal had to do with it, I realised that I probably should have ducked, because that was when I received the blows that split my left ear, my nose and my forehead.

'No, the other injuries are from rolling round in the gutter.'

As I said, I am not naturally given to violence, but, 'Well,' I was thinking, 'If that's what he does with his white stick, then a) he doesn't need one, and ought to have his benefits withdrawn, b) he should be charged with carrying a dangerous weapon, and c) there's a more appropriate place where he might keep it.

'Could you roll up my sleeves, please, Gertie?' I asked my carer.

Reporting restrictions on the case of the Black and White Traffic Lights incident – as it has been dubbed – have been lifted today. Here's a special report from our legal correspondent…

Reports on the social media, including graphic footage of the incident, have been checked by experts, including our own. Internet exposure has generated massive interest on the social media from AzUlikeIt to Zee!, and many news-sharing outlets.

'Additionally, many eye-witness accounts have been taken into account,' police say. They now confirm, 'The incident *did* take place exactly as the footage shows; it was unaltered.' One particularly distressing clip has been shown in its five-minute entirety, receiving fourteen million hits Worldwide, averaging one million per day.

'The event is believed to be heading for record viewings on YouTube, although we can only show a much-abridged clipping of it here.' So said that Soapy woman on BBC.

'This was the core event of the encounter, in which one of the protagonists took the white cane off the other, and "Performed an act of insertion", as Mr Dillywhite, leader of the Senior Surgical Team explained. 'This was an unprecedented act, in my experience, with approximately seventy centimetres of the cane being inserted into the body of one of the persons involved. That's a little over two feet for we decimal-phobes.

'Police have admitted that they are unable to separate the two antagonists with regard to blame,' Soapy on the News was saying. 'In the interests of public good, charges of violent public affray against both participants have thus been withdrawn. In a face-saving compromise for the police, both assailants have agreed to accept an official warning, although the actual responses by both persons are not repeatable before the watershed.

'The individual who had initially been standing at the pedestrian crossing waiting for the Green Man, is said to be a Mr White, a former SAS sergeant. It is believed that he is currently in the Bahamas on a holiday, thought to be paid for by a spontaneous crowdfunding reaction on the Internet. Sufficient funds have also apparently been raised to pay for the repairs to his prosthetic legs.

'The other person involved has been identified as a Mr Black, who has moderate visual impairment in one eye only. It is rumoured that his allowance and benefits are currently being reviewed. He is reported to be still recovering in the Nottingham Queens Hospital, where it is believed that the removal from his body of the white stick was particularly difficult as it is formed of twisted cane. It also had a large reinforced rubber ferrule on the end. This has not yet been recovered. If nature does not take its course in the next few days, hospital sources say, another operation will be required.'

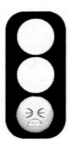

THE AUTHOR

Trevor is a Nottinghamshire, UK writer. His short stories and poems have frequently won prizes. He has appeared on television discussing local matters, and his photographs frequently form the background to the BBC weather forecast.

As well as the New-Classic series of SF short stories, he has published two books in the OsssOss series of short stories about people and places just around the next corner.

He has also published many non-fiction reader-friendly books and articles, mostly about the volcanoes he has climbed around the world; and dinosaur footprints on Yorkshire's Jurassic coast.

He spent fourteen years at the classroom chalkface; sixteen as headteacher of a special school; and sixteen as a government (Ofsted) school inspector to round it off. His teacher wife now jokes that it's "Sleeping with the Enemy".

In the 1980s, his Ph.D. research pioneered the use of computers in the education of children with profound learning difficulties (so it's *Doc* Watts, actually).

BY THE SAME AUTHOR

SCI-FI — OF OTHER TIMES AND SPACES

The Giant Anthology of Sci-Fi stories. 460 pages with 39 tales of here and now, and the futures that await us.

- If you were spying on another planet, would you do any better than Dicky and Miriam in the snappy two-pager "Air Sacs and Frilly Bits".
- Could you live among the laughs and lovers of "I'm a Squuumaid"?
- Or cope with the heartache of "The Twelve Days of Crystal-Ammas"?
- A tentacle drifts across your naked form one dawn... are you having Second Thoughts about this relationship?
- Are you sure it's not your fault, what happened to the moon?
- Daisy's got her fingers stuck in the Popcorn Machine? So what?

★ ★ ★ ★ ★

"Sci-fi at its most original"
"Absolutely excellent, equal with anything I have read in the genre, including all the old masters."
"Great entertainment; good stories from start to finish."
"A sci-fi feast – I highly recommend it."

Book 1 in the New-Classic Series of Sci-Fi from the Lighter Side.

AMAZON READER
REVIEWS

"Loved the sheer variety on offer"
"A great book of short stories to delight any sci-fi reader's palette"
"Go on, give yourself treat!"

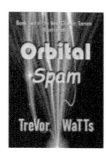

Book 2 in the New-Classic Series of Sci-Fi from the Lighter Side.

AMAZON READER
REVIEWS

"A great selection"
"A heads up on this third one I've read by this author"
"My kind of real characters – I get their humour and dilemmas and problems and solutions – or failures, sometimes."

Book 3 in the New-Classic Series.

Book 4 in the New-Classic Series.

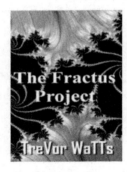

- <u>So</u> you have an affair with a Tangerine, but did you expect this to happen?
- Morris was desperate for Fame, but *this?*
- Can Mz Dainty possibly pass her space pilot driving test amid so much chaos?
- In the next three minutes, can you call the right shot when the enemy's High Space Drifter comes barrelling towards you?
- As the death toll mounts along the old Brinsley Mineral Trackway, why don't the police have a clue?

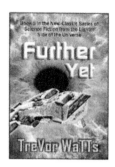

Book 5 in the New-Classic Sci-Fi Series.
To be let of the leash in 2021.

- Under interrogation, would you give them the secret of Vondur'Eye, regardless of the consequences?
- What comes shimmering along the beach?
- Effo the maths genius has forgotten... what?
- Your ship's suffered a breach – Severity Level 1 – so where does your future lie now?
- When you're the Store Boss in the hold of an interstellar merchantman, there are some things you *Really* Shouldn't Do.
- Is this the right attitude among the officers of the SN Destroyer "All for One"?
- Why did the workshop drawer keep closing itself?
- Could this be a whole new slant on Starry Gazey Pie?

Non Sci-Fi Books

Twists & Turns
OsssOss1

Thirty-five short stories (not Sci Fi),
critically reviewed as "Terrific",
"Superb stories."
"There's nothing routine here."
"Very, very readable."

- In Quiz Night, can she answer the ultimate question?
- Does Baksheesh Bill want to save the life of the enemy pilot?
- The *Prim* Reaper? Who are you kidding?
- There's more to this lady than Three Silver Buttons.

Taking it Personally
OsssOss3

- Thirty-five short stories about the things that people do.
- What The Boss said was most regrettable, but he has to live with it.
- Would Uncle Dave allow the thieving creature into his cardboard castle?
- You think you're in the cells for a night? Think again.
- When United win the cup, *everybody* drinks with them. Or else.

**(Still toying with the title.
May well be "Go You or I")**

234

Worlds of Wonder – Book of Poetry

Collected poems that everyone
Can see themselves reflected in.
Of flower-strewn girls, of ponies gone,
A ranch-hand wreaks the deadly sin.

Filling up the parting glass;
Of cats and men and ladies, too.
World War One and graves en masse;
Of dynamite and the Devil's brew.

Machu Picchu and Galway Town
Whoever said Old men don't fall?
From Java's mud to nature's gown
The pages here unveil them all

Minimum Arrestable Delinquency;
The haggis that truly took my heart;
In elegant idiosyncrasy
I take my leave, I must depart.

A FEW NOTES

These stories each have their own back-story, and I feel very attached to them all.

Get'em all Dad was the result of three hours in a traffic jam in Nottingham when the Clifton Bridge was suddenly closed.

The A42 – happened very much like that.

A Near Miss was the first story I ever read out to my local Writers' Group.

Audrey Hepburn… I saw someone much like her in another car in heavy traffic. Eyes met. Smile and finger-wave. She was gone.

Cold Nights in Canada is so true – up to the meteorite. We couldn't decide if that bloke was a laugh or a pain.

Diversion – actually took place in Namibia, though not quite to that extent.

The Aringa Desert Walk – an Aussie friend told me about a tradition he and some mates had. Sat-Nav Sadie crossed our path in Brisbane in 2014. Isobel is Waiting – very few liberties have been taken with my portrayal of the Aussie police. If only I'd been Isobel…

They Flee from Me, and Cinda was in one of her Moods, were written when we were walking the Appalachian Trail in 2019.

High-Baby was a weird-looking conversion we saw in Texas; and the Brass Kettle Diner really does exist, just outside Tucson, with a slight change of name. If you go there, you'll recognise it at once.

The Causeway was inspired by a break we had on Holy Island, Lindisfarne. Chris, my wife, was convinced I'd get the timing across the causeway wrong.

Igor was once employed locally, under a different name.

Oh, yes – Lioness. Closely based on an Egyptian guide we had on a Nile cruise (our first holiday by air, also our first cruise, and first time to Egypt). Except he was a man, and he stopped short of mass murder, as far as we were aware.

Every one a treasured memory – TrevorW

Credit for the "Buster" quirkon goes to:
dreamstime.com/majivecka_info

Contents, covers and titles of future books – beyond the next one or two – are subject to changes, whether whimsical, or necessary. Such as if I've written a story that I really like, or is particularly topical, so that leaps to the front of the queue; or if I find or take a more pleasing photo for the front cover; or if I can't trace who holds the copyright for a picture I've been using on the book-construction site; or if a better title appeals to me Such as Go You or I, instead of Taking it Personally, Or Personally Speaking – You wouldn't believe how many titles I've tested on covers for that one.

Printed in Great Britain
by Amazon